A MARRIAGE TALE

Charles Denby

Janet Steve —
Blessings
Love Charley

PublishAmerica
Baltimore

First printing

ISBN: 1-4241-8205-0
PUBLISHED BY PUBLISHAMERICA, LLLP
www.publishamerica.com
Baltimore

Printed in the United States of America

He said to me, O mortal, eat what is offered to you; eat this scroll, and go, speak to the house of Israel. So I opened my mouth, and he gave me the scroll to eat. He said to me, Mortal, eat this scroll that I give you and fill your stomach with it. Then I ate it; and in my mouth it was as sweet as honey.

—EZEKIEL 3:1-3

EVENING

The Falks, Adam and Marion, were unpacking. A light sea mist enclosed them.

"Do you want me to build a fire?" he asked.

She scarcely heard. From the time when she had first observed her father exhaling smoke into soap bubbles, Marion had found comfort in feats of encapsulation. She had achieved as much with Adam, swathing him in layers of indifference. "It's late," she replied. "There are extra quilts if we need them."

Arms outstretched, Marion stood at the center of the room holding a lamé top in the attitude of a dance partner. Predecessors that had already had their audition with her hung neatly in the maple closet nearby. Even in this remote spot, he thought, she needed to project a Connecticut swank, an aristocratic shimmer; to do so was to maintain a state of hopeful preparedness—for the grand moment, the fairytale event that would redeem her ennui. "That's a nice color on you," he praised.

"You've always liked me in blue, haven't you?" she mused, spinning on one heel to face him.

He concurred. She had worn mostly denim when he first knew her, a coy brunette idling away the first year after Sarah Lawrence on her uncle's ranch outside Aspen. His fondest memories of her were set in azure, linked to the hues of earth and sky he had discerned in the soft play of her chestnut hair against her blue-jeaned body. "It suits you," he replied.

"It did," she said, "when I was an optimist. Black is more my color now." She regretted this barb instantly. Her relationship to Adam resembled an old house succumbing, gradually, to decay: as long as nothing was said about it, they could both affect a genteel disregard for its condition; the enunciation of any flaw, however, called for a reflex effort at patchwork. "I'm sorry, Adam," she confessed. "I know you worked hard to make time for this trip. I'm just sorry Jack and Susan had to back out: they're such a kick!"

The week they were about to spend had been conceived, half in jest, the year before. The four of them had sat on the beach grouped beneath a *Cinzano* umbrella. Skimming the classifieds in someone's *Alumni Weekly* or *Monthly*, Susan, intrigued, had read one aloud:

Maine seacoast. Four bedroom cabin on private island.
Full utilities. Recently renovated. Dramatic views all around.
Available for rent May-September.
Inquiries: Box 4404, Haverford, PA 19041

A wonderful idea—let's—they had all casually agreed. But three months later their memories had to be prompted when Susan called with a report: the arrangements were all set; it was theirs for a week at the end of June; all that was needed was a deposit. They had both been too flattered to demur; as a couple, this form of approbation had rarely been bestowed on them. Stoically, they had mounted little objection when their friends later called on short notice to beg off— *of course we understand; of course we'll give you a rain check*— since, as confidences were inevitably broken and word of their troubles spread, they had anticipated fears of contagion, a polite but incremental ostracism.

"I'm afraid we're marooned, darling. Just think of me as your Caliban," he quipped, executing a flourish.

Lured by this gesture, she studied him skeptically. Just past forty, Adam's body was acquiescing to the force of gravity: already he exhibited a slight stoop and a perceptible sunkenness around the eyes and mouth; age was subtracting some of the military correctness from his appearance. Offsetting this, in the summer his complexion turned engagingly Mediterranean, a uniform tone of mellow bronze. "Well," she asked, "does this beast know how to make a nightcap?"

"Most certainly, madame. I will provide."

Relieved by a momentary sense of mission, Adam grabbed a flashlight off the dresser and slipped away into the unfamiliar night. The real estate agent, Mrs. Judkins, a breathy and obsequious woman who had accompanied them on the launch out from Bass Harbor, had surprised them with the news that a pre-stocked liquor closet came with the rental. He navigated toward this now, sleuthing down a sconce-lit hallway that featured, along one side, a kind of commemorative mural. Here, mostly framed, were ancestral portraits, group pictures, cocktail invitations, dinner menus, skeet scores, badges, buttons, and more. Before the week was up, he knew, Marion would examine every item on this wall, attempting to cull, from a determined study of all their bric-a-brac, an inductive knowledge of the owners. Beyond the hall he came to a massive oak stairway serving the center of the house where, correctly, he turned left, found a light switch, and entered the living room.

Modified A-frame, he observed. In college he had considered becoming an architect. The quiet harmonies of design, the prospect of conceiving a whole into which all parts could be snugly and cleverly fitted, had appealed to his penchant for order. His dabblings in the field had enduringly shaped his perception, for often, when he first viewed a room, he first assessed what lay behind the walls, and only secondarily what lay within. His take on this space was vertical: from the high-peaked ceiling, down to the beveled pine shafts used as beams, then the lordly granite fireplace. *Solid. No corners cut. Must have taken years to construct.* Only in afterthought did he discover the décor: the sprightly mint-and-teal upholstery, the Art Nouveau lamps in frosted glass, the supine seals conceived as ashtrays. *Probably have great parties here,* he thought, locating the bar behind a pair of folding doors. *Good taste in booze, too. Bushmills will do nicely. Stoli for her. Such enlightened people. Honor system. Just tell us what you've used.*

By the time he returned, Marion had slipped into an off-white nightgown and into bed. Propped on two pillows, she was reading *Emma.* Along with her cool, arch manner she had inherited from her mother a need to retreat, at therapeutic intervals, into the past—into a world of muted appetites and gracious gestures. Far away to the west, he imagined this self-contained pose being echoed by Julia Scott, who, in widowhood, had acquired the habit of retiring early to a bed-chair. Marion's father, sportsman, collector, and habitué of Chicago high society, had been dead nearly five years now. His passing had been tidy, an event already discounted by the ebbing of his wits, and apart from agreeing to take on a night nurse, Mrs. Scott had shown little outward evidence of being affected. Derivatively, such stiff-upper-lippedness, a trait common to all the Scotts, disturbed him. At his own funeral he pictured a nucleus of intimates convulsed with grief, a corona of bleary-eyed well-wishers. In pain there is remembrance: narcissistically, he wanted the bonds he had formed with people to tear at them after he was gone. "What have you got for me?" she asked, her eyes still trained on the book.

The question was posed distractedly, in a voice devoid of inflection. Her regal mode. The ease with which she was able to narrow the scope of their interchanges, withholding the conversational riffs that so charmed her friends, pricked him. In return he offered ambiguity, a suppressed retort. "I think you'll be pleased," he predicted, setting her glass down on the night stand.

Turning away, he began the motions of undressing, pulling up his shirttails with his free hand. Getaways like this, to distant venues, tended to spark his eroticism. Conscious of this while unbuttoning, he pressed his palm against the taut plate of muscles developed on the playing fields of his youth and then, imagining this touch to be female, extended it slowly out over the knob of his shoulder. For a man, his skin was unusually smooth; his former loves—six in all—had been unanimous in their appreciation of his texture.

"Do you think we should call the kids?"

Her query, projected with unexpected amplitude, startled him; a sip of whiskey washed onto his thumb. He licked this up, savoring the

8

pithy taste it made in combination with his flesh: spiked bouillon. "I think it's better to give them a wake-up call." Naked to the waist now he turned again to face her, to display his tensed and ready paps, to increase the menace of his physique. "About noon. You know how they are."

The Falks differed from most of their friends in having married young and in having produced children promptly thereafter. Already they were empty-nesters—David would be a sophomore at Trinity, Sarah a junior at Brown—liberated from the ritual collaborations of parenthood, the fetters of basic obligation. Their freedom, however, came at the cost of ambivalence; generally, they envied the many couples their age who were still busied furnishing succor, still anchored in the domestic hubbub.

"Don't remind me," Marion pleaded, sighing. "We probably should have gotten a house sitter." In her mind's eye she beheld their home as it would appear in the wake of a bacchanal. "The Barnacle" was a brown-stained, cedar shingle set on one of the last buildable sites before Chafee Point, towards its end, became an immense stony talon gripping the Atlantic. She and Adam had stumbled upon it fifteen years before, during an investigative foray down the South Shore; they had instantly adored its elevated decks and porthole windows, sensed the potential for some heightened form of intimacy beneath its narrow gables and low-hung ceilings. One of the oldest homes in Quidnunquit, it was also one of the most admired. Its improbable survival through the generations, its willful endurance in the face of countless nor'easters, had made it iconic, an emblem of the kind of briny tenacity the villagers aspired to recognize within themselves. With ownership, thus, came obligation, an unspoken code requiring that its residents uphold its virtues: chiefly pluck and perseverance. Through strenuous efforts on the tennis court and creditable performances in 420 regattas on the Massachusetts Bay, she and Adam had strived to meet this standard, or, short of that, garner approbation for trying. Genetically, however, they had failed to pass along an instinct for appearances; free spirits both, their children disdained country-club rankings and yachting honors.

"I told David I would deduct the damages from his allowance."
"No! You didn't?"

To sustain the dialogue he had tapped a sure source: her protectiveness for their second-born. In the third week of life David had been diagnosed with pyloric stenosis, a palpable anatomical flaw which had caused her mother's milk to dam up, undigested, at the end of his stomach. Although a simple operation had led to an immediate cure, the experience had left its mark; ever-after she had retained an anxious need to give her son more rope than he needed, more tolerance than he deserved. Derisively, he reminded her, "The kid's a slob, Marion. He has no concept of property rights. In the course of a week he could destroy the place."

Baldly put, yet the point was valid. David's capacity for dexterity declined along a centripetal gradient: his mind could balance, manipulate, and react, but his extremities could not. The more intently he studied or polemicized, the more soda cans and pizza boxes toppled. Last fall, over parents' weekend, the detritus in his room had been ankle-deep. "Relax, Adam," she countered dismissively. "Sarah will keep him in line."

My honey-haired darling, he thought, recoiling into the bathroom. He had tried to be a chauvinist—prefer his male child—but failed. Psychologically, he was more aligned with his daughter, disposed towards a moral and existential reflectiveness which, in David, appeared stunted. They were linked, also, by physiognomy: Sarah had his long face and olive-green eyes; she possessed the same sleek limbs and soft-footed gait. In the simple, weather-filmed mirror he inspected their shared features. In Sarah some vital part of himself seemed to have been rolled forward in time, reshuffled, improved. The decisions she would soon make weighed on him as if they were his own. Would it be foolish to get a Ph.D.? Was there room in the world for another classics scholar? Or would it be more practical to go to med school? Subtly, he had tried to advocate for the latter, not because it was more traditional or more secure, but because he prized most in her what he frankly and ironically lacked: a natural, unstudied warmth. "I hope so," he called.

A MARRIAGE TALE

Retreating further, he closed the door behind him. *End of conversation* he thought, relieved. They did not talk *to* each other, but *at* each other. Failing to craft a harmony with their words, they now aimed merely to be clever or correct. The loser in this game of one-upmanship would likely lose confidence, would struggle to make a life beyond the marriage. Examining the twin bays of exposed flesh above his temples, the baleful pouches below his eyes, and the sprig of grandfatherly whiteness arising from his breastbone, he rendered a recurring judgment: it would be him.

There were candy canes, she recalled, and oddly grinning teddy bears and plumpish dolls with pigtails and little gift boxes adorned with green ribbon. They had floated on a field of blue so close to the color of sky, especially in winter, that she had imagined, when very young, that some tier of the atmosphere, or perhaps heaven, was also like this. By the time she was reading Dickens and Twain they had repapered her room in an abstract, a-thematic pattern, but this was long after the imprint of those original, fanciful images had set in her remembrance. Often, in her mind, she returned to that space, slept alone in her old canopy bed, lulled by the distant low rumblings of the late evening rail traffic running north, out of Chicago. Tonight, however, she could not obtain any purchase on the past; this raw June night, populous with unfamiliar scents and sounds, commanded her vigilance.

He would be coming soon: her incubus. Finished with her chapter, she awaited him in the chill, moonlit room, burrowed beneath the covers. In recent years the process through which they sought communion had become inverted. Uninvited, he would steal upon her in the dark, making his way up through the bottom of the sheets, navigating along her calves and thighs with a lolling tongue. In some ineradicable recess of her imagination she exhilarated in the notion of having him bend before her—grovel—and this ascending method of seduction sometimes approached that conceit well enough to succeed. Still, when she yielded to him in this way it was passively, as a stricken creature: he had become venomous to her; where he touched it, her body felt weightless and numb. As he lowered himself onto her she had learned to float away and then, for the rest of it, just spectate: look on as he applied himself to her in a wanton canine frenzy and, with a queer feral ending cry, tore away his meal.

Once, he had been her prince. Unaffectedly, she had called him that during their courtship, culling the term not only from Princeton, where he was completing his last year, but also from oblique impressions of his ancestry, which had seemed, in an American sense, royal. In Adam's lineage there were senators and ambassadors, admirals and poets. A great-great uncle had once run for president; a second cousin had served on the White House staff. The Falk genes, arguably, conveyed an instinct to strive for distinction. The promise of this, the prospect that she might be able to mingle her chemistry with the stuff of statesmen, had drawn her to him; hers, by contrast, was a family of loafers and ne'er-do-wells, otiose inheritrixes skulking in the shadows of a remote ancestor, suffocating on his compounded wealth. Strolling along the hushed cloisters and cobblestone promenades of that magical campus she had been enchanted, dazzled by the hope of release from the humdrum; this boy, she had conceived, would lead her away from complacency, from a smug, inward little life played out at the end of a commuter line. Onto his chosen field of medicine she had grafted her own ambitious dreams: he would be a surgeon—a famous one—and walk on the world stage; in the early years they would be itinerant, as his training took them to the major medical centers in the great cities; later they would settle on the North Side and become leading citizens; their children, four in all, would be fair-haired, enterprising, and substance-free.

She did not know, exactly, when she had begun to fall out of love with him. We register our exultations acutely; our disappointments, by contrast, are mostly cumulative, forming soft edges in the landscape of memory. At some point after they had decided against having more children, his presence in her life had become less a necessity, more a given. At that stage she had permitted herself to accept the deception that this was part of the normal evolution of marriage, that the fruit grows mostly after the bloom; the untempered affection she had once felt for him, she surmised, had pooled with her love for David and Sarah, and with maturation, had grown more diffuse. Subsequently, throughout the long middle years of parenthood, from training wheels to driver's ed, she had allocated that amount of attention to Adam which seemed his due. By the same dynamic of obligation which led her to feed the dog, sop up spills, and answer cries in the night, she had soothed the cyclical ache in his loins, comforted him just enough. But the part of the copy she could not overwrite was boredom. Adam had become an internist, not a surgeon; a practitioner, not a professor. He had joined an established group in Hingham, intending, professionally, to live happily ever after. While their neighbors had attained rank or founded enterprises, he had humbly tended their viscera, countering the agues and anginas, the eructations and dyspepsias which accompanied their successes. Gradually she had grown tired of their tidy, predictable existence and tried to flavor it. Together they had joined paddle tennis groups and book clubs, taken cooking instruction and dance lessons; alone she had studied Native American history and practiced tai chi; finally, at her insistence, they had entered therapy. But despite her best efforts, Dr. Rosen, a grandmotherly Wellesley graduate with an office off Beacon Hill, had not been able to reinvent them, for unlike her more workable cases, they did not bicker foolishly nor commit abuses or fumble at sex: their behavior did not require modification. And despite all of her training and experience, Dr. Rosen knew of no cure for *la nausée*.

For months she had been thinking of leaving. Had some recognizable terminus—a finish line—appeared, she would have sprinted to it by now. But in marriage, she knew, we undertake a journey marked only by intermediate milestones. To reach a surcease one of them would have to drop by the way, quit. She had already explored the dreary mechanics of doing so, consulted an attorney, and solicited advice from a handful of divorcees. She was poised to act but lacked the will. It was the quality of her breeding, she supposed, which prevented her from deconstructing their wedlock. Traditionalism and competitiveness were woven into her character more deeply than she had imagined. *Never give up, never give in; for better, for worse; 'til death do us part.* Her conscience would not let her reject these baked-in credos.

Closer now to the verge of sleep, she pictured a gilded seascape. In their living room, set proudly above the fireplace, hung a painting of the Newport shore, circa 1890. Within it a population of beachgoers clad in period costume was depicted. Some of these lazed on the sand; others, younger or more vigorous, frolicked near the water. As if through magnification she glimpsed two of the latter, a couple gamboling in a tidal pool toward the left edge of the canvas, and with a low moan, inaudible to her, recalled a comparable scene, life imitating art. *That evening in Nantucket. Me fetching wrack out of the surf, slipping it slyly down his trunks. He clutching more, giving chase. The cove in the rocks where he caught me, a place out of sight. Then falling with him to the still-warm sand. And the sea-grasses pressed between us. Making salty love in the dusk. Panting. Laughing. Murmuring...Oh.*

Her face, he saw, bore no expression. It intercepted the world indifferently, without seeking an effect. *My angel,* he thought. *Where have you gone?* The evenness of this sleep, unaltered by the night's imperfect blankness, had always pleased him. Once he had accepted it as testament to her happiness; now he took it as nothing more than sound repose.

Her body, lithely distributed into the posture of a sidestroke, lay still and unprotesting as he slid in next to her. These last few minutes of the day, while he waited to join her in oblivion, had become a balm to him. In this small interval they remained at ease with each other, or he could pretend as much. Here was untainted space; here their antagonisms ebbed.

Could there still be hope for them? Hardly. Not long ago he had tried to take the measure of her antipathy for him, cataloguing all the defects marring the figure she had once adored. The result had been a monstrosity, a loose-bellied, foot-slapping, hairy-nosed, knock-kneed, odoriferous, hankering, inconsiderate, underachieving, overserious, sometimes effeminate misfit: him. Ever since, he had tended to hold her blameless for the erosion of feeling between them and for the detached, almost clinical way she touched him, when she did.

He had not been a Pygmalion to her, either. As his wounds had accumulated, he had sunk to wounding back. With stray, then heedless, then intentional snipes he had chiseled away at her unselfconscious native spirit, guided her towards a fickle and doubting vision of herself. That was the cruelest part of a failing marriage: insidiously, you stripped each other of the power of self-deception.

In the polyhedral space between them his fingers crept forward, finding a ribbon of her hair. Silken. Like the edging on a baby's blanket. Insensate to this encroachment she became, again, a player in a scene cast by his memory. Overhead, gulls wheeled and, in the foreground, the jubilant shrieks of small children punctuated the steady hiss of the sea. They were at Horse Neck Beach. Or was it Scituate? Or Marblehead? Before Sarah, they had spent summer weekends exploring the coastline between Kennebunk and Sakonnet. In their imaginations the Atlantic had seemed a vast, complex jewel somehow capable of reflecting and enhancing their passion, and in endeavoring to view it from as many angles as possible, they had had a sense of constructing a metaphor about their relationship, a theme of quest they could both endorse. On such days they would lie at the foot of the dunes, paperbacks in hand, coyly awaiting the thinning of the crowds, the onset of dusk. Finally he would signal her with a cue such as this, whispering, "Come here."

How long had it been, he wondered, since her flesh had been animated by fondness? Now, when their bodies met—during the occasional, reluctant sexual interlude, or even, quite simply, when he attempted an embrace—he encountered a substance something like marble. Age had not altered her skin's exquisite softness, but, beneath it, a hardening had occurred; her musculature had become armor, a shield against him. In turn, he had become an opportunist, a sneak, almost a *frotteur*; while she slept he canvassed her anatomy for pliant tones, some semblance of welcome. Skimming the underside of the sheet, his fingers traced a low arc through the dark, descending, stealthily, to her abdomen. He held his breath and awaited a rebuff, but none came. Below her waistline he cupped the slight matronly roundness where, he imagined, her favorite hors d'oeuvres and bonbons came to rest. Once she had been indifferent to food, to the art of cuisine, but in recent years she had developed an interest in gastronomy that seemed almost hormonally driven. In their home the sense of clutter—of completion—previously furnished by the scatter of children's toys was now sustained by a profusion of culinary accouterments. Somewhere in the sloppy alchemy of the kitchen, in the archetypal motions of mixing and stirring, in combining pabulum with pabulum, she had discovered a source of fecundity. To cook was to create.

On the drive up the coast they had stopped at a restaurant offering, on its signboard, the default rural promise of, "GOOD FOOD." After sampling the local microbrew with him Marion had lunched on sliced turkey, peas and carrots, and corn bread. Unaccountably, he began to contemplate the fate of this bland meal, this ordinary sustenance, in its journey down her alimentary tract: the delicately minced mouthfuls tipped back into the esophagus, plummeting, blending with each other in the stomach to form a rank slurry; then, beginning in the duodenum, the nutrient tide of amino acids and carbohydrates, molecular whirligigs breaching the cellular shores of the intestine, becoming the substance of her; finally, the obscene remnant, that which would not become her, snaking its way lower and lower, arriving at her cloaca. Coprolalia: they had not tried that. Abruptly he understood it appeal. Utter prostration. Absolute veneration. But how to perform it, exactly? Should he lick it or—mercy!—eat it? *Sorry, dearest. That I wouldn't do, even for you.*

In the distance, through a lower window pane, he discerned a pair of pinpoint lights. A car on one of the larger islands, he surmised. Somewhere a dinner party was breaking up. Accomplished husbands and their adoring wives were turning in. Some would soon make love;

others would simply laugh and review. All would feel contented and companioned, securely embedded in the goodness of life. Such was his usual, envious assessment of the lives of other couples: uncritically, he accepted the stories they chose to tell about themselves, the presumptions of piousness and monogamy they strove to create. Constitutionally he remained a Pollyanna. In this he was the beneficiary—or the victim—of his parents' marriage. For forty-four years and counting, the union of Ed and Louise Falk had proven unfailingly cinematic. From their seemingly scripted courtship, conducted while he was a football star in traction and she was a blushing candy-striper, through the verdant decades spent rearing sons and exemplifying normalcy, to the brink of dotage, they had remained vitally linked to each other, inseparable and indivisible.

As a child and even as a young man, Adam had taken this oneness, this effortless and affecting symbiosis, for granted, believing the geometry of all marriages to be sturdy and equilateral, assuming his would resemble theirs. Instead, the configuration of his wedlock had quickly turned asymmetric. From early on he had had to placate and inveigle Marion. Some untraceable hurt had made her fear a balanced connectedness with him—or, he judged, any man. When she spoke to him it was with ellipsis; when she came to him it was after negotiation. *We might play around later,* she would grant, *if…*The ifs were about authority: more for her, less for him. *If you'll follow my lead. If you'll take my word for it.* As a consequence their relationship had taken on the character of a strange, sad waltz. Step-by-step he had entrained her with apologies and deferences, always moving backwards, habitually giving ground.

Adultery—the Faustian alternative—had tempted him for years. In his imagination he had had affairs with most of the women in Quidnunquit, tasted the muffs of neighbors and dinner partners, schoolmarms and shopkeepers. Through a series or moral self-inoculations he had prepared for a suitable opportunity, convinced himself to construe the event, when it came, as a reward, not a lapse. But in those aberrant and breathless moments when a possibility seemed to present itself, at the point of inflection into undue familiarity, he had always refrained. In each of us there is a strand of will, a recurvature within the conscience, which we underestimate. In Adam this was a pert and native idealism, a soldierly determination to hold the line, which made him unable to violate any pledge or commitment, particularly his vows.

A faint sweet sound, more than a breath, less than a whisper, passed Marion's lips. Some wish being fulfilled, some satisfaction attained. Gauged by the tone of these exhalations there was a Proustian quality to her sleep. He liked to think that she spent most of it strolling through rose gardens and apple orchards, taking high tea with ladies in bustles. Of necessity, these hours and their set pieces, the downy creations of her unconscious, had become a refuge: at the edge of desperation the mind seeks its quotient of relief. *I'm sorry dear,* he wanted to say. *Once, it was so right. Do you remember that day on the trail, our horses resting, when I first drew you near? Such a fair thing you were; such a fine love we had. So sorry to have botched it. Never thought I would.*

Chancing that caresses could convey promises, he let his arm roam. Again he was sixteen, his fingers diffident in their advance. First, he found her navel, still snug and sunken after all these years. Then up onto the shelf of her sternum: such a natural place for a man to dock his hand. Here he felt the surprising labor of her heart, its thudding beat reverberating through her ribs. He yearned to reach in and reset its rhythm, heal; or, like a clock, perhaps he could rewind it, turn it back to a time predating the first disappointment he had dealt her. This sojourn across her chest, he wanted to tell her, was not intended to be erotic; its conception lay in the meager hope that subliminally, he might effect an apology. But on the up slope of her breast a second hand came over the back of his, ushering it away.

"Don't," she said.

MONDAY

Again she was soaring. This had always been the only dream she could recognize as such, and not, in so doing, end it. Emboldened by this awareness she spread her arms wide and, catching all the breeze, sailed above the treetops. She relished this moment especially: when you first broke above the grip of Earth and had a view. Here she felt free.

The topography was rural. Below she saw fields and silos, hedgerows and elm-shrouded streams: a Midwestern vista. Her unconsciousness seemed to rebuke a seacoast setting; for its venues it preferred the heartland, carrying her back to those uncrowded spaces, the checkerboard landscapes she had known as a child. And proudly so: the ocean beneath her was as vast as any other. Effortlessly she rode the currents above it, catching eddies and uplifts, ascending the ramps and spirals of summer air.

We are all creatures of place, questing to return to where we set out.

After a time, or half a time, she came into a nullity, a featureless zone. Here there was neither arrest nor motion, neither presence nor absence. Here she floated beyond the planet's pull. But if weightless, then airless. Too high! Vainly, like Icarus, she had risen too high! Above her a light appeared; on her skin she felt its gathering warmth. She tried to retract her wings—descend—but a magnetic force seemed to attach to her chest, hold her up. The light grew brighter, nearer, and she began to flail, reaching for a strand of gravity. It must not end like this! There was so much more to teach the children, more to—

"Scottie?"

Out of the firmament, a voice spoke to her: a god? From Zeus or Apollo she would not have expected such a reedy timber.

"Scottie—"

"Mmm?" The sound of her maiden name, converted to the diminutive, put her on guard. Only Adam used this sobriquet.

"Good morning!"

Between the two of them he had always been the earlier riser; his sleep was somehow denser, capable of completing its work over a shorter span. As a consequence he had acquired the habit of stationing himself in a nearby seat and keeping watch over her until she woke. In their early years she had scurried through the reentrance into consciousness with a childish eagerness, anticipating that he would be there to minister to her with coffee, a caress, and often a fresh-cut blossom. But as their bond had thinned the sweetness of this custom had commensurately faded; now his morning vigil seemed disproportionate to their affiliation, a voyeuristic act.

"What time is it?" she asked, muffling a yawn.

Why should we care? he might have posed. For the next seven days they would be deprived of appointments and obligations, work and volunteerism. The set routines that, at home, buffered them from one another, would be lacking. "About eight," he guessed. "Did you sleep well?"

She had begun to employ props—a retainer to curb bruxism, a tummy-pillow to impart security—to sustain her night's rest. The pillow, in displacing him from the more useable side of her, had become a rival; pathetically, he perceived opportunity in the fact that she had neglected to bring it along. "Well enough," she sighed. "It *is* cooler here."

Here he imagined a concession: many of their best memories— Bermuda in April, the Vineyard in October—had been recorded off-season. For them, a chill in the air ushered in hopeful associations. Rising, he approached the window opposite the foot of the bed and assumed a wistful contrapposto. *Six panes upper and lower,* he counted. *No storm frame. Must put up boards in winter.* "It's going to be a splendid day," he predicted, peering out. "While you're getting up, I think I'll scout around."

"My brave husband!" she extolled, mimicking the effete Victorian wife.

Impelled by her sarcasm, he retrieved a paint-splattered sweatshirt from the dresser and went out. Through a French door in the hallway he exited onto a small deck and, from there, down to a vestigial path. The view was northwesterly, from an elevation of no more than sixty feet. The outer islands of Penobscot Bay, recumbent green leviathans, cluttered the horizon. His mission, he decided, was to reconnoiter the area around the dock, assess the recreational infrastructure. Clambering boyishly over granite slabs and ferny crevices, he took an impromptu route directly to the shore. No more than a quarter of a mile in length and half of that in width, the island was just large enough, for these latitudes, to support vegetation. Scant deposits of soil in the low places yielded a piebald growth of juniper and scrubby stands of pine; closer to the water a fringe of goldenrod thrived. Though stark and weather-beaten, the place bore enough of a living mantle to be hospitable. His own ecology, he reflected, was similarly precarious: without Marion his life would be barren; sparse though they were, her softening womanly touches made his days bearable.

The sea, where it met the land, was grayish-green, a murky jade. Offshore, darkening shades of blue, aspiring towards sapphire, marked the transition to deeper water. Just above the high tide line Adam discovered a band of smooth stone, the polish work of storms. He followed this at a strolling pace, tranced by the lapping and soughing of waves, the hiss of brine; behind him, the sun, still in the early stages of its climb, highlighted a loose array of fair-weather clouds. After passing two small wrack-strewn coves, he came to a larger inlet, the sides of which were extended, at right angles, by breakwaters. In the middle of this concrete-and-granite maw, its shape suggesting a stubby tongue, a short dock protruded; beyond its reach a sloop and a powerboat drifted on moorings. Inland, a welter of smaller craft—Sunfish and sailboards, inflatables and dinghies— rested on trestles. *No shortage of toys here,* he concluded. Jealously he pictured the sportive scenes that would transpire in July and August: the owners and their friends setting down their drinks and diving off the gunwales, a troupe of raucous children cavorting in the waters around them.

He and Marion had never had a second home. Ignoring her petitions, he had been late to grasp the restorative potential of an alternative locale, a Campobello. They could have afforded a house on Sunapee or Winnipesaukee, but this would have required the use of Marion's money—more of it. Already, she had funded their equity in the Barnacle, vouched for the children's tuition, bankrolled roof repairs and redecoratings. Yes, it was nice to have married a rich girl, but only up to a point; beyond that his self-esteem pivoted on his ability to reject the marginal luxuries, in refusing, as a husband, to be kept.

His first footfalls on the metal ramp leading out to the dock clamored unexpectedly, flushing a pair of gulls. In the course of his walk he had managed to lose himself slightly, but in creating this commotion he lapsed back into pained self-awareness. During the weeks and months past he had tried, in anticipation of their parting, to adopt a no-fault philosophy of divorce: couples failed because the relational adhesive, the "chemistry" between them had aged and attenuated; or because, as with garment and wearer, the fit had changed; or because it was an existential imperative, their entelechy. Now he renewed this effort, laboring to construct within his mind an absolving syllogism, a logic of forgiveness; yet, as always, he remained a moral determinist, insistent on laying blame. *You just didn't live up to your billing,* his conscience decreed. *She wants—deserves— something better. Time to let her go.* But what would he do with himself, after? From medical school to practice, from betrothal to empty nest, his life had coursed along predictable channels; in a divorce he would be sluiced out, mere spillage, into the cold gulf of middle age.

Treading lightly, he advanced to the end of the dock, the limit of his excursion. At the edge he sat down, dangled his legs, and let moroseness overtake him. "In my end is my beginning," he recited aloud. *Wish I could believe that. You were more resilient than I,*

T.S. No strength to start over. Easier not to. Might try to balance the ledger, at least. Take a boat out. Loop the anchor line around my neck. Jump. No mess. Difficult to make it look like an accident, though. Sorry about that, darling. Insurance companies hard to fool. But the kids and you—
"Here you are!"

Our better judgments are often made acutely, when we least intend to make them. Turning, he saw Marion and bestowed, upon himself, a bittersweet benison: he had been right to marry her; she was a beautiful woman, finely rendered. At forty-three she retained a girl's litheness, a balletic poise; instinctively, she passed agilely through space, nearly tiptoeing, as if entrained in some game of stealth. The mechanics of her body, transparently observable through her summer clothing, were deliciously sensual. For years he had delighted in watching her reach for a forehand, arch to pull in a halyard. Even now her muscles' supple cooperation, their easy movement beneath her pampered skin, enchanted him. "You know me," he said. "I gravitate toward water."

She acknowledged him with a faint wince, a brief curling of her upper lip hitched to an aborted wink. Rarely, these days, was she able to face him without exhibiting signs of conflict. "I tried to go back to sleep," she told him, "but there was too much light."

"They should think about putting shades in."

"I'll leave a note suggesting it."

An arm's length away, she sat down next to him, legs over, also. Unlike many women her age, she was comfortable being viewed in profile; apart from a slight sagging below her jaw and an emerging tendency, inherited from her mother, to cup her shoulders inward, time had imposed few modifications on her physique. She was still fair, quite marketable. "Whatever became of us, Adam?" she asked, tossing her hair back and bracing her hands on the dock.

The readiness of his answer surprised him. "I don't know. We just don't seem to understand how to be together anymore."

Facing away from him, she closed her eyes and rehearsed the justifications for a break-up. Though most of his charms had gone flat for her, a few retained their potency; she continued to treasure his giddy mischievous laugh, his level, deep-set gaze, his unassuming disposition. She had yet to discover a way of factoring out these residuals. "I don't hate you," she offered. "I just don't feel what I should for you."

As he mulled this statement, parts of their habitat seemed to weigh in with an indecipherable commentary. A sudden gust of wind urged the pines into a chorus of whispers and fanned the wave tops into a fine palpable spray. "It would be too artificial to court you again," he said. "I just don't believe in this idea of 'dating' your spouse."

She could not recall Dr. Rosen suggesting this; evidently Adam had delved into the self-help literature. She was touched. "Let's not blame each other," she advocated. "People who do that remain bitter."

"No, I agree. Being sad is enough."

"We just *fizzled*, Adam."

"Yes...yes, we did."

Finding this image of lost effervescence a just metaphor, an enough-said, they lapsed into silence. He scanned the close-by water for a congress of minnows; she perused the heavens. From appearances they would have been judged content, a couple complacently unwinding. In fact, it was their lowest ebb, their blackest moment. Abject and helpless, their marriage lay in their arms like a diseased child who has failed all treatments, whose time is near. Yet there was the rub: we never surrender our children. They must be torn from our arms. Fate alone can claim them. The Falks had not been able to reconcile themselves to the injuriousness of a split; neither one had achieved complacency about exposing the kids to the consequences of a divorce. A review of the psychiatric studies had not helped. The bottom line: their division would beget future divisions. Scientifically, what would be best for David and Sarah was a well-played charade.

"This isn't a bad place to spend a week," he resumed. "We should make the best of it, enjoy it for what it is."

She admired this segue. The doctor in him was coming out: palliation if not a cure. "I agree," she echoed limply. "I'm surprised there are so many flowers still in bloom. Have you ever seen so many asters?"

A MARRIAGE TALE

About a mile offshore, Adam noticed a small powerboat that seemed to be heading right towards them. *Constant bearing, decreasing range.* He loved nautical terms. Uttering them selectively in the company of the old salts, the wizened dockhands and naval-officers-turned-yachtsmen whom they encountered along the waterfront enabled him to feel remotely a part of the military brotherhood, a league of competent, adequate men. "By the way, did you invite someone over for breakfast?" he quipped.

"Hmmm?"

"The boat out there is coming in our direction."

Squinting, Marion peered out at the distant hull bucking the chop beyond the breakwaters. "Maybe he's coming to pick up a pot."

Adam looked for the high prow, the jumble of rusted equipment in the cockpit. "I don't think so. He doesn't look like a lobsterman."

Jokingly, she proffered another theory. "This must be how they deliver the mail up here."

By now, Adam was beginning to make out detail. "If that's the case, they're using child labor." The craft, a center-console runabout perhaps twenty feet in length, was being piloted by a diminutive figure in a blue baseball cap. It irked them that so many parents could be so casual about the hazards of boating. Here was another adolescent—if that—left to run amok in the family whaler. "It looks like a kid out for a joy ride," he told her.

They watched impassively as the interloper made his way closer. Soon the whine of the engine was audible, then the staccato thwacking of stern against wave. The helmsman, they perceived, had a leathern look; he was not a youth.

As he approached the mouth of the inlet he put out fenders and acknowledged them with a salute.

"I didn't expect to be pitched out here," Marion snapped under her breath.

"Wave back at him," Adam exhorted. "Look friendly."

"I'm always friendly, Adam."

"Yes, I forgot: you're never brusque."

As the boater entered the harbor they saw that he was elderly, a jowly, rail-thin little man, attired in a green plaid shirt and khakis.

"He looks like an elf."

"We should be glad he's a Cubs fan," Adam said, recognizing the familiar red C. "A sorcerer is just what they need."

Wary of chicanery, they rose and prepared to catch the lines. The visitor slowed and maneuvered along the dock between them, tossing the bow lead to Adam, the stern to Marion; he cut his engine and then, with what seemed like incongruous alacrity, hopped up unto the deck. "Good morning!" he greeted in a twanging voice. "You must be the Falks."

Adam stepped forward as their spokesperson. "Yes, and you are?"

Bent over a cleat, the stranger seemed not to hear. "I hope I'm not too early. You folks must be tired. It takes longer than most people think getting here from Boston."

There were no dropped R's in the man's speech, Adam noticed; he was decidedly not a local. "That's right, but perhaps you could—"

"All set now." Finished checking the tie-up, the boatman rose and extended his hand. Catching the sun, his pale eyes reflected a luminous, silvery color, a lunar sheen. "My name is Clarence Ross. Please call me Clarence."

As they shook Adam made his grip unnecessarily firm. Though he towered over the older man, he felt the instinct, in this isolated spot, to present an imposing front. "I'm Adam," he said, "and this is Marion. Can we help you?"

The newcomer displayed a canny smile. There was something dimly ambisexual about him, the sort of preciousness typical of men who have frequented both sides of the avenue. "In fact, it is I who come to help you."

"Oh?"

"I come to be of service—to act as your personal chef."

So that's his game, Adam thought. *Of all the places to be solicited.* "Thank you," he said, "but I think we can manage on our own."

The stranger allowed a pause to develop, and unaccountably, within this small interval, their apprehensions began to subside; they felt themselves ease into a balmy and unfounded sense of familiarity with him, a premature confidence that his intentions were benign. "It is not as you are thinking," he resumed. "There will be no need to pay me."

Adam glanced at Marion, invoking her assistance. She had a knack for sizing people up, for swiftly plumbing character. "I think you need to explain to us," she said, "just what it is you're proposing."

"Of course, ma'am." Ceremoniously Clarence doffed his cap, revealing a bald head, oversized for his body, that was as tectonic, as chiseled, as any work of Rodin. "It's really quite simple. For the week that you are here, I'll be preparing all your meals. Breakfast and dinner will be served at the table, lunch picnic-style. I'll use what you've already brought and procure whatever else is needed. I'll be on the island mornings and evenings for a couple of hours; otherwise you'll have your privacy."

In her mind Marion discerned a type. There was, about this man, an acquired classiness, a studied poise within his role, that could only mean one thing: surely he had been a professional steward, a manager or barman at some oaken, exclusive club. He had retired up here and worked occasional private assignments. Perhaps the Brahmins had stinted on his pension.

In his mind Adam weighed risk against reward. On one side he placed his wife's diamond-and-sapphire engagement ring, a smattering of costume jewels, and a small amount of cash; on the other a week's relief from kitchen work and the entertainment value of this little troll. The scales, he decided, balanced narrowly on the side of taking a chance. "And why would there be no charge for this?" he asked.

As he answered, Clarence's features seemed to widen, as if straining with an effort of nondisclosure. "I've been sent to you," he said.

"*Sent* to us? By whom?"

The oldster regarded them with a knowing, almost paternalistic expression. "You may discover that, in time."

"It's okay, Adam," Marion interposed, assuming a peremptory tone. "I think I know who's behind this." *Judy,* she thought, *you shouldn't have.* With her best friend she was engaged in a one-upmanship of generosity. Three summers ago she had taken in Judy's two adolescents so she and her husband could take a trip to Italy. A week of Mr. Ross's attentions must be her recompense. Her friend had really done her homework on this one.

"Sweetheart, did you tell my parents where we are?"

True, it would have been in character for Adam's mother to put something like this on; she was one of those overly energetic and unabashed women with a penchant for expressing their affection grandly, by arranging events for people—clamorous birthday celebrations, stagey costume parties, madcap weekends—that they would never dare orchestrate for themselves. To blunt the impact of a divorce, however, she had already tapered her connections to Lu-Lu: their weekly telephone chats had become biweekly, then monthly; the flow of e-mail between them had been stanched; their sojourns to Saks and Bloomingdale's had been curtailed. To have mentioned this trip to Lu-Lu—so idyllic, so implicitly romantic—would have been contrary to her purpose, a false signal. "It's a marvelous gesture," she said, dissimulating. "Someone we know wants us to be totally at leisure. I don't think we should disappoint them."

"You're right," Adam accepted. "Why look a gift horse in the mouth? We'll find out soon enough who masterminded this."

"Then it's set!" Marion bounced girlishly on her toes. "No cooking for a week, right, Mr. Ross?"

"Clarence, please."

"Oh, Clarence, you're such a darling! We're so glad you've come!"

The affinities that most of us feel towards others comprise a spectrum: at one end are the few raffish souls who have earned our dislike; at the other that precious handful whom we love almost unconditionally; and in the middle, a vast acquaintanceship whom we favor by degrees. With Marion, though, there was little shading of relationships; either they were richly colored in or they were abandoned as sketch work, unworthy of further development. From her trilling, exuberant pitch and the vivid flush welling in her cheeks, Adam knew that Clarence had been sorted into the first category. Here was a work-in-progress, her newest, dearest friend.

"If it's agreed, then," Clarence continued, "I'll bring what I need up to the house. You folks haven't had breakfast yet?"

"No, we—"

"You must be famished! Fresh air whets the appetite, doesn't it? Twenty minutes: I'll have everything ready in twenty minutes." Enthralled, they watched as the little chef scrambled back down into his boat and rummaged for provisions. His movements were remarkably limber for a man of his age; he showed no hindrance from stiffened sinews or aching joints. Momentarily he was back on the dock holding a small wicker basket covered by a white linen drape. "I think that's all I'll need for the moment," he declared. In his mien there was something puckish, a pinch of mischief; he appeared to be savoring some tomfoolery that was part of his mission.

"The kitchen is a little bit primitive," Marion warned.

"Not to worry, Mrs. Falk; I'm highly adaptable. As you were, then. I'll have everything ready shortly."

And with that Clarence sallied down the pier, up the ramp, and onto the path leading inland. When he was well ashore they held a hushed conference.

"Adam?"

"Yes?"

"What do you think?"

"I think he's a miniature Ike."

"What?"

"Eisenhower, the chief executive before J.F.K. He's an exact likeness." The caricature seemed apt. It was quite conceivable that this self-assured little filbert of a man had been in the service at some point, perhaps as an adjutant, a minder of ceremonies, a keeper of protocol. He had a touch of officiousness to him that could easily have been left over from a career as an aide-de-camp.

"This is no time for jokes, Adam."

Philosophically he disagreed. On the wards he had always admired those peers—surgeons and procedurists, mostly—who understood how to diffuse anxiety with humor. "Very well," he replied, "let's examine the possibilities. He's not psychotic, I doubt he's a criminal, and he certainly doesn't represent a physical threat. Actually, I rather like him."

"I do, too. He's so cute!"

"And this story of his—that someone hired him—*is* plausible."

"Of course: plenty of people could have set this up. It might be Jack and Susan's way of apologizing for finking out on us. Or one of your mother's crazy initiatives. The kids might have even decided to do something nice for us. Whoever it was probably just called up the real estate office and arranged it through them. With so many tycoons and bluebloods summering in these islands, I bet there's a whole slew of Clarence Rosses hanging around, available to cater to their every need."

"Well, someone had a stroke of inspiration."

"We might just as well play along and enjoy it."

"Why not? For a week we'll live like the Lodges."

The long hand on Adam's watch pointed to the seventeenth notch on the bezel. It pleased him disproportionately to have discovered an above-water application for his favorite timepiece, depth-tested to six hundred feet. Marion had long ago stopped imploring him to remove it, in preference for something dressier; that she permitted him to wear this bulky, often incongruous object on his wrist, even in the most formal settings, provided a wisp of hope: in loving someone we submit to their idiosyncrasies. "I think it's time to go up," he announced, funneling his voice through cupped hands.

Knee-deep in the brine, Marion was prospecting for crabs. "I can see them skittering around," she declared. "I'm going to come back at low tide and bring a net."

"You should have been a biologist," he told her as she heron-footed out of the water. It would not have surprised him to learn, from some omniscient source, that his wife had spent more of the past two decades tending to animals than raising her own children. Not only had they housed a plethora of pets (five dogs, seven cats, schools of fish, and one Angora rabbit, cumulatively, to date); she had also taken in a succession of maimed and dislocated creatures, most recently a wing-shot duck, found floundering on the beach last fall, which she had patiently nursed back to health. Yet, increasingly, it rankled him to observe these ministrations, confirming, as they did, that the well of tenderness within her, the nectarous font from which other men might soon draw, remained undepleted—indeed, brim full.

"I probably would have enjoyed it," she admitted, hopscotching along the gaps in the rockweed. "I like to paw around in nature; I'm obsessively inquisitive." Suspended between love and enmity, they had reached, it seemed, a temporary equilibrium, a transitory state of peaceableness, which offered a gratuitous benefit: for once they could trade objective commentary, unvarnished advice. "We complement each other in that respect," she added.

"How?"

"The universe isn't grainy to you, Adam. Where it isn't necessary you don't care to know the details."

"It's true," he conceded, jumping down from the boulder where he had perched. "I have no wish to comprehend auto mechanics. I just want the car to run."

Back on terra firma, Marion bent over to roll her pant legs out and clean the wrack from her shoes. This was one of the alluring paradoxes about her, that she was equally at home sauntering through an art opening or wading around in muck. Shortwinded, she continued, "I'm sure that's part of the attraction I felt for you. You're so beautifully impractical."

"I never liked that aspect of myself, though. I think it's why I wanted to go to medical school: I was trying to compensate."

"Thank goodness you chose a specialty that's not mechanical. For you, orthopedics or plastics would have been a scary proposition."

"I would have turned out a lot of crooked limbs."

"Or ugly noses."

They were conscious, remotely, of probing for a voice, a reservedly affectionate, bantering, yet measured tone that would work for them in the thereafter, in the derivative relationship that would emerge after their marriage had become emotionally unrecoverable, after prurient interrogatories and compulsory testimonies had opened an impassable gulf between them.

"Primum non nocere," Adam quoted. "First, do no harm. At least I know my limits and stick with them. I'm a prudent man."

The adjective cut. Was what she was about to do prudent? She was a woman on the verge of leaving her physician-husband, her cozy social life, and perhaps, her seaside residence—for what? For a supposition, a conceit; for the vain assumption that she would be able to swap into a better package. It would give her her just deserts to end up recoupled to a wife beater or a womanizer; there were plenty of cads out there lying in wait for a woman of means, a plush mark. "You're sensible," she confirmed, touching her fingertips to the angle of his jaw. It was an opaque gesture, part conciliatory, part dismissive. Under the strain of misery, our behavior fragments.

"I like to think so," he managed, accepting her dubbing.

She withdrew her hand and, for an instant, an interval which could scarcely be endured, they stood at an uncomfortable proximity to each other, like two people who have been jostled together in the subway. And in that interminable brief moment they both felt it, what every couple fears more than rancor or, even, infidelity: a deadness, much of nothing. After twenty-one years of marriage there was no charge, no sensual spark between them; reciprocally, they had become indifferent. Mercifully, Marion found the impetus to break it off: "Let's see what our new cook has been up to."

When they reached the house they discovered a table set for them—white cloth, floral centerpiece, napkins folded into origami waterfowl—on the screened porch that wrapped around the living room. "This is a good sign," Marion whispered, taking a seat. "He cares about presentation; he's probably been to culinary school."

From the direction of the kitchen they heard a medley of clanking and scraping sounds.

"He certainly sounds busy," Adam commented, alighting beside her.

"That's encouraging also: good cooks bang around a lot; they're uninhibited."

Waiting for their server to appear, they defaulted to scenery-gazing. Across the island's ragged silhouette they had a view of the eastward sea, of coastal-cruising sloops and the offshore commercial fleet. "We should have brought the boat up here," Adam lamented.

"It would have been a long run."

"We could have put in along the way. Who's that friend of yours in Newburyport?"

"Pam."

"Right. We could have stopped to see Pam for the night."

Early in their marriage, neither of them would have suspected that pleasure boating, among all the effortful distractions pursued by the empty-nesters, would prove the one to snare them. What little Ed Falk had known about watercraft he had unapologetically failed to pass along to his two sons. Manhattan-born, for Adam's father a round of golf or a sortie onto the squash courts had constituted a sufficient nod towards outdoorsmanship. Marion had had more time afloat—weekends on Lake Geneva and summers in Charlevoix—but the entirety of this had been spent as a passenger; in a hands-on curriculum she had been a hands-off student. In the brackish towns of New England, however, to own a boat was practically de rigeur; accepting this, they had obtained a slip once the children were able swimmers, and the next year, diffidently filled it. That had been three boats ago; now they owned a twenty-eight-foot twin outboard, *Memories.*

"The rental agreement says we can use their boards and skiffs."

"Yes, that was good of them."

"I think I saw two Sunfish in the racks. We can have a race around the island."

Always so competitive, he thought. *Part of her still a tomboy.* In school she had captained the soccer team, excelled at lacrosse. Arguably he had erred in marrying an athlete. Jocky women more obstinate than most. "I might just beat you," he retorted. "I read a couple of chapters on racing tactics last winter."
"I'm impressed. It's not like you to study a sport."
"Sailing's different. There are so many subtleties, and not all of them can be deduced."
"VERY WELL," a voice blared, "I think we're set to begin."
Turning, they saw Clarence at the tableside, even though the racket in the kitchen, or its echo, seemed to be only just subsiding.
"For your breakfast," he continued, with unremitting nasality, "I have orange juice, blueberries, oatmeal, or scrambled eggs, and fresh bread."
It would be an adjustment, they both realized, to have to listen to that awful tone for seven days.
"I'll take the oatmeal," Adam specified. "My cardiologist wouldn't have it any other way." The comment was prankish, self-mocking. He was guilty of the common vanity among younger physicians: he had not yet yielded the care of his body to a peer.
"The eggs for me, please," Marion said. Approvingly, she had taken note of the fact that Clarence had donned a full-length white apron that appeared freshly laundered. He had been contracted through an agency, she surmised.
The bantam chef confirmed their orders with a nod, then withdrew. When he was out of the room, Adam made a last attempt to figure the odds of treachery. He pictured the headlines—"Massachusetts Couple Killed on Private Island," "Coroner Investigates Foul Play in Vacationers' Deaths"—but his best efforts to conjure suspicion failed. He could not manage to feel imperiled by this water-born gnome; the improbability, the convenience, the preposterousness of the situation had begun to charm him, like a spell. "I could get used to this," he sighed, setting his weight back in his chair. "There's something to be said for letting yourself be pampered."

"Someone believes we deserve it," Marion mused, inspecting the flower arrangement. *Tiger lilies,* she observed. *All the right touches. Better than the average room service. The only thing lacking was a British accent.*

"I've been going over the list of who it might be. There are quite a few possibilities."

"We're not unpopular, dear. Externally, we don't do badly as a couple."

"This is quite a time to be arriving at that insight, isn't it?"

They were rescued from moroseness by Clarence's return, the gentle clatter of china. Their breakfast was laid out for them, with full formality, off a japanned service tray. As would be their experience throughout the week, the food was competently, if not exceptionally, prepared; the berries were stemmed, the eggs fluffed, the oatmeal sprinkled with cinnamon. If there was anything questionable about his work it was decidedly the bread, which he unveiled with a curious bit of ceremony. "Take, eat," he said, retracting the cloth covering a small wicker basket.

Marion served herself first, taking a slice of the pre-cut loaf. "Mmmm!" she opined, when the morsel had cleared her palate. But it was mere politeness, feigned appreciation: What she had tasted was insipid, a substance uniquely devoid of flavor.

"Incredibly filling," Adam commented, referring to its peculiar denseness.

Thus even in their disaffection the Falks adhered to the niceties: to spare an old man's feelings they took care to check their opinions.

After the meal, they decided to explore. Half a dozen trails fanned away from the house; they chose one that led southeast, across a shrub-packed hollow. The sun was now well up in the sky, and the island had begun to retain its heat. In the brake they felt this warmth below their waists, a layer of static air pooling beneath the sea breeze. For Marion these conditions provoked a memory of mischief;

replaying it as she walked ahead of Adam, she felt her lips curl into a sly, self-amused grin. On a day hotter than this, staying on after a wedding in the Adirondacks, they had found themselves hiking through similar terrain. On a whim, she had pulled off her top and bra; unslung and bare-chested, her breasts immodestly bobbing with every uneven stride, she had promenaded half a mile or more until, lust-crazed, pleading for release, he had pulled her down. When they were done, lying sweat-soaked on the forest floor, she had given him an instruction: "You may call me other names, but never a prude." *If anything gives a woman power over a man,* she thought, *it is the willingness to stage an atavistic sexual act.* Even today, she held certain productions in reserve.

Beyond the glen, they followed the trail up a gradual rise to a small, open plateau; traversing this they came to a rugged bluff, a maritime panorama.

"Land's End!" Adam announced.

Before them stretched the vast, scalloped plain of the outer Bay. Dozens of vessels—single and double masts, trawlers and fishing charters—studded the tableau. They had not expected to find these waters so frenzied with traffic this early in the season.

"Let's find a place to sit," Marion suggested.

Acceding, Adam led them down a short descent, locating, within a shallow crevice, a suitable shelf. They settled here, their backs to the rock, communing wordlessly with the view. "I'm sorry I misrepresented myself to you," he intoned after several minutes had passed.

"Don't—"

"No, I need to say this." For emphasis, he put his hand on her shoulder, applying a light but importuning pressure. "I let you believe that I was made of better stuff than I was. I was manipulative. I let you fall for the uniform."

"I did have a thing for white coats."

"I should have let you know more about who I was, inside." Penitently, he turned away from her and crossed his hands in his lap. "You probably thought I was more like Peter."

"Heaven forbid!" she gasped. Two years older than Adam, Peter Falk had always cut a sharper figure. She had met them together, two skinny boys affecting manhood, at a cocktail party in Carbondale. Peter was taller, fairer, and smarter; even then he had displayed a guileful, predatory edge. In the presence of women, married or not, he exuded a frank and unapologetic lustfulness, an unseemly willingness to engage in concupiscent deal-making. Divining a stunted moral architecture beneath the wit and the charm, Marion had never liked him; his most prominent failings—two divorces and a rebuff by his first law firm—were condign, she was sure.

"But I know that my brother has made my father proud, and I haven't. I couldn't admit that before now, to you or to myself. I've been pretending all these years, putting up a front of adequacy and hoping a few people would believe it. I'm tired of the whole charade: I am what I am."

While he was speaking, Marion had been struggling to contain a twin confession. "Stop, Adam!" she pleaded. "I put you up to it; don't you see? You married 'a Scott,' into an 'important' family. My parents never let you forget any of it: how much influence they had, how many boards they sat on. They set you up to compete with my brothers, who had it all given to them."

An image of his wife's brothers, configured as a diptych, loomed in Adam's mind. What she claimed was true: They had been just as caustic as Peter to his self-esteem. George, the older one, had gotten the looks; an athlete at Groton and Yale, he seemed to skate through life with the same effortless strides that had once carried him up-ice. As a broker he had been a natural, leveraging the family name into a fat client base, a crowded social calendar. Harry, four years younger, was more cerebral. After consigning his twenties to travel and epicure—an indulgence—he had dabbled in journalism and, subsequently, publishing; now he was a consultant and defender of causes, known on a first-name basis to many in the environmental leadership. In the swaggering and puffed-up atmosphere of the North Shore, Adam had been overmatched against George and Harry; he had lacked their ability to subsist osmotically on wealth and power. "You're right," he accepted. "That's why we left Chicago."

"But I never warned you. In those days I was just like them. I took everything for granted: the money, the parties, all of it. I didn't marry you, Adam, I adopted you. I assumed I didn't have to give anything up."

"'I was going to be a 'society doctor.'"

"Exactly."

"And we were going to live in Lake Forest."

"Or Winnetka."

"Did I fool you, or did you fool me?"

"We fooled each other."

This conclusion, so starkly unearthed, prompted, after a delay, a mutual reflex. She tittered; he chuckled. Then, together, their souls shrugged something off, a layer that had been binding them, and they roared: laughed as long and hard as they were able, settling into an almost antiphonal rhythm, cycling through rounds of crescendo and decrescendo. Eventually Adam composed himself sufficiently to express a corollary judgment. "At least we're finally being honest with each other."

Marion drew a deep breath, and audibly exhaled. "It's refreshing," she admitted. *Very.* In a week's time, she conjectured, they could carry this discussion to completion. She had heard of people being "happily divorced." What was necessary, evidently, was iron-clad certainty, exhaustive proof; by confirming all that was irreparable between them, by coldly cataloging the advanced state of their marital disease, they could demonstrate, reciprocally, that it was hopeless, and from these paired conclusions draw a contradictory peace of mind, an actionable resolve.

"When we met," he continued, "I was naïve. I thought there was something special about being a physician."

"But what you do *is* special," she insisted, her voice inflecting ardently. The slant of his personality, she believed, had predestined Adam to a medical career. He lacked the effrontery, the steadfast egotism of a businessman; his adaptation to the world was receptive, feminine. "You help people."

Looking askance, he saw that she had turned towards him. Often, when she wished to make a point between them, she would cock her face at angles like some pert, curious bird and wait until their gazes met. He had always found it difficult to respond to this gesture; her eyes were so clear, her irises rendered in such an ethereal shade of blue, that in training his own upon them, he felt impure and unworthy. His confession, however, had left him with a sense of expiation; for the moment, he was able to regard her unflinchingly. "I'm glad you appreciate that," he said.

Marion brought her arms up and clenched them around her chest. "You're lucky," she said, hunching over as if to squeeze out some ache, some unexpurgated misgiving. "You'll have something to do afterwards."

"They say it's important to keep busy. If I feel low, I suppose I'll just work more hours."

"For me, it's not so simple. You can go on being a doctor, Adam, but what do I do? I was brought up to be a socialite."

And quite successfully, at that. His memory reprised a vintage scene: newly engaged, they had been given a dinner at her uncle's summer retreat, a constellation of private islands at the west end of Georgian Bay; in a close-weave emerald dress she had chit-chatted her way through a roomful of corporate higher-ups and their pedigreed wives. He could still hear the reviews: *She's such a dear! So precious! Good catch! Keep a tight hold on this one!* "You could sell real estate," he suggested. " It's practically the same thing."

"But I didn't want to sell real estate, I just wanted to be m-married." Her face blurred. When Marion cried, she did so tastefully, constrainedly; she had learned to hold sadness mostly within her, releasing it, when it came, in a series of muffled exhalations.

"We both did," he said, putting his arm around her, drawing her in.

Few of us employ a multiplicity of confessors. Though, at times, we may confide in ministers, counselors, or friends, it is necessarily with something held back, the raw amniotic stuff at the center of our being. This we know how to release only to our mate, our bed partner, if to anyone at all; with them alone are we able to achieve a full catharsis.

Setting her head in the hollow of his shoulder, Marion mourned this aspect of losing him; now she would have no recourse to an abiding listener, no secure place to psychologically undress. "I'll miss you," she whispered, pressing her palm to his breastbone.

Preserved within this simple touch he glimpsed the old Marion: sweetly affecting, soulful, intuitive. How untimely. He would have preferred not to encounter this untainted version of her while they were being disjoined. Helplessly, he responded in kind, echoing the sentimentality. "And I'll miss *us*."

"That's enough for now," she protested, breaking away. She felt suddenly nauseous, gripped by his "us." He had pronounced the word in the exact way necessary to tear at her heartstrings; the sensation was insufferable. Their leaving each other, she realized, would have to be a process effected through repeated small dosings.

"You're right. Let's leave it alone for a while."

Accordingly, in silence, mulling this partial exegesis of their failed love, the Falks rose and retraced their route back to the house.

Children cry out, arthritics moan, hypochondriacs bring lists. As a race, we are rarely hesitant to announce our discomforts; yet the reverse does not obtain. When our bodies are in proper working order it is not our inclination to confirm it. Though we may gasp at the pleasure of slipping cold-skinned into a warm bed, or hum our approval after tasting some particularly savory dish, we do not, as a rule, express appreciation for the subtler grades of well-being. Thus while the Falks may have swapped observations concerning the unexpected glories of their locale—that the periwinkles were so abundant, that the petrels could be seen flying so close to shore—they did not, during any of the desultory conversations they had that afternoon, choose to remark upon the unaccustomed change that each detected inwardly. Perhaps they attributed it to the sea air: this apprehension of lightening, this loss of avoirdupois. Perhaps they believed that, when there is an emotional letting-go, the body produces a matching sensation, the perception of a burden eased. Or perhaps they made no attempt to fathom it at all. For naturally, if we are weary, and the chance to rest comes, we do not reject it; inevitably, we sink into it, let it be.

"You're from Michigan, aren't you?"

They were finishing dinner: tuna steak and glazed carrots. By Marion's estimate they had dealt long enough in superficialities; it was time to pry.

"Very good, Mrs. Falk. I grew up in Lansing—how did you know?"

"Oh, I'm from the Midwest myself. I recognize the accent."

Amusedly, Adam joined the interrogation. His wife would not stop, he knew, until she had ferreted out the man's entire biography. "That wasn't a Tiger's cap we saw on you when you arrived."

"I have an even greater fondness for the Cubs, sir. Their appeal is universal; they emblemize the human struggle."

"They generate so much pathos."

"That, as well as bathos."

Clarence had been refilling their wine glasses during this banter. Marion admired his poise, his ability to parry wits while attending them. She supposed that he had received training in one of the great hotels. Exploring this notion, she asked, "Have you always been a cook?"

"Not at all, madam. For most of my life I could scarcely boil water."

"Honey, did you hear that? There's hope for you yet!"

A novel theory bloomed in Adam's imagination. Perhaps it was his wife who had hired Clarence: as a going-away present she was giving him a cooking coach, someone to instruct him in the rudiments of cuisine. "I doubt it," he retorted. "No Falk male has ever felt at home in front of a stove."

She sidled past this tweak. "So, how did you become interested in working with food?"

"The One Above pointed me in that direction, it seems."

Intellectually, if Adam and Marion shared common ground, a subject on which their opinions energetically reinforced each other, it was on the issue of religion. Both were determined agnostics; they placed no more faith in Jesus than in Santa Claus. Yet it was also their habit not to confront the assertions of believers; a polite attentiveness to the claims of the worshipful was, for them, a necessary civility, an appeasement owed to simpler minds.

"That was good of Him," Adam said.

"Or *Her*," inserted Marion.

"It's true," the runty chef expanded, "I never expected to be blessed with a second career."

"What was the first one?" This was Marion's method in plumbing a life: she preferred to bypass the subheads.

"I was a teacher."

"Really? What subjects?"

"Grammar and composition to all, literature to a few."

"You were an English teacher?"

"No, they knew English by the time they came to me; I taught them usage."

Adam's consciousness veered off into a queasy association, the sense of *déjà vu*. Throughout his life his self-concept had been sculpted—diminished—by captious, clever men: first his father, too much the attorney, for whom every conversation was a draft contract inscribed in space; then, at Deerfield, the curmudgeonly duo, the two sententious masters who had accorded him C's, requiring his family to exercise what remained of their pull to garner an acceptance to Princeton; finally and most destructively, all those Socratic intellects he had encountered in medical school, a white-coated legion of sharper minds. But if Clarence was no less quick-witted than these other figures, he was not as acidic, as invidious. A week of jousting with him might prove decent sport. "Modern or correct?" he quipped.

"Some people—*like*—don't know the difference."

"Here, here!" Their server raised the claret in salute. "America is becoming a nation of illiterates; there seems to be no stopping it."

"Turn off the computers," Marion suggested. "Without spell check they might have a chance to learn."

"That would be thinking outside the box!" Adam cracked.

"The teachers' union wouldn't stand for it," Clarence lamented. "They want the software to do all the work for them."

"Where did you teach?" Adam asked.

"Mostly around Detroit. I also had a stint in Cleveland. I never left the Rust Belt."

"What grades?"

"High school, all levels. Everything from syntax to Shakespeare. But enough about me. How was your day?"

"We didn't do much," Marion confessed. "We took a short walk."

"We shook off some stress."

Again there was a gap, a missed beat, in the dialogue. It was not so much a flaw in the conversation as an enhancement of it, a rhetorical lever. And within this space they now surely sensed the workings of an inexplicable benevolence.

"Marion?"

"Yes?"

It was nearly dark. To the east the twilight had culminated in a succession of lavender, then violet tones, an infiltration of mawkish colors into the lower heavens. After dinner they had migrated to the seating arrangement at the opposite end of the porch, two wicker chairs bracketing an all-weather settee. Throughout the vacation they would generally spurn the plusher appointments of the living room: as a pair in turmoil they felt more appositely positioned close to the elements, the fickle and variegated moods of air and light.

"Since we're at this stage—"

Every proposition has its prologue. He was convinced that there would soon be movement between them, a release from the prolonged inertia they had been floundering in. Even so, there should be no requirement, at least initially, that they break camp. They could declare a limited open season before the mail had to be rerouted. For some couples a period of experimentation, a sampling of the alternatives, led to the final decision, pro or con. *What would you think,* he was close to saying—of what? Of swapping. Becoming swingers. How to phrase the question? *Of a little exchange. We'll call it double-dating.* The Gladfelters, he was sure would oblige. Betty always generous with the innuendo. And Harold stealing a bit of mouth-on-mouth every time they greeted. A lot of hostility between those two. Must also be on the verge. Harold was barrel-chested, hirsute, powerful: probably give Marion a excellent shagging. And Betty his coequal: sturdy, big-breasted, a veritable Rhinelander. Appropriately, they were not that fond of Harold and Betty. More acquaintances than friends. You wouldn't suggest such a thing to people you really cared about.... In truth, it hit him, they couldn't suggest it even to the Gladfelters. "Since we're at this stage," he recommenced, "I want to thank you for giving me two wonderful children."

Marion settled back into the upholstery, her postprandial slouch. She had feared that he was broaching some grittier subject: alimony or equitable division. Later, there might be need for that. But for now they shared the gathering dusk, this lustrous vista. "I thank you also, my husband," she said. "That much, we did well."

Adam had neglected to bring a book on the trip. So rarely, in fact, did his readings reach beyond the scope of disease management and the daily news, beyond glycoproteins and geopolitics, that he had half-forgotten the comforts of fiction. By default, as they lay in bed awaiting the summons of sleep, Marion having rejoined the adventures of Miss Woodhouse, he contented himself with an imaginative study of the ceiling. In his fancy the knots in the pine had become planetary bodies suspended in a tawny galaxy and he an astronaut piloting a gleaming ship through uncharted space. *How pleasant,* he mused, *to think again with a boy's mind. Easier to invent worlds than live in this one.*

"Doctor Falk?" She called him this, most often, to forewarn of a conversation that was going to be businesslike, to-the-point.

"Yes, nurse?"

"There's something I want you to know."

Seeing that she kept her book upright and her eyes on the page, he braced for a sobering disclosure. In her grimmest moods she held to a brittle aloofness. "What is it?"

"I don't think of you as a failure."

"Just something less than a success?"

"And I won't talk you down to the kids."

"Thank you." It would be a true kindness, he thought, if she kept this promise. Too often, women played out their advantage after a breakup; they leveraged the primacy of the bond formed primordially, at suck.

"A lot of couples do that," she continued. "They behave badly. We shouldn't."

Here, a last plus in having married a patrician: He could trust her to usher them through their marital Gethsemane with an admirable graciousness, and afterwards, on the sparsity of occasions that would bring them together, she would set a tone that was nonchalant, rinsed of resentments. Their divorce would be artful. "I agree," he said. "I'm sure we'll both be fragile for a while; backstabbing won't help."

Glancing sideways, sighting along the edge of her paperback, she viewed him furtively. Sorrow did not register frequently on his face; when it did, it carried an astringent force, causing him to purse his lips and blink prolixly. The take she obtained now was inconclusive; he had turned his head away. Was it odd, she wondered, that she should need to observe his pain? Was it perverse or improper, at this point, to confirm that he still loved her? "It's funny," she said, "I think this trip will be good for us. It will give us a chance to work through things."

"Kind of a reverse honeymoon?"

"We'll save on attorneys' fees," she predicted.

"Now there's a source for sweet dreams."

Thus cued, Marion closed her book and reached for the light. Sighing, she said, "Let's see."

TUESDAY

*Between sleep and wakening: these straits I loathe to pass.
Here my thoughts roam unmoored, adrift on fractious seas.
Where are the wrens? Or is it vireos? That little mincing sound
I hear at dawn. Whatever happens, I need a garden. More so than
a man. Second marriages more work than the first. Tending what
others have planted. Step-children. Step-pets. Lives grafted onto
lives. Not organic. Still, a girl can't help noticing what's out
there. Michael Hoffman. Cute buns. Great hair. I know he looks
at me. He's henpecked, for sure. Maybe he'll opt out some day.
Or Peter McAllister. Those dark eyes. Something about the way
he held me at the Christmas dance. A little too tenderly, a little to
long. Most of them still think I'm pretty. Thank God for cosmetics.
But would they like all of me? Varicose veins starting to show.
Nothing's as tight as it was. And the Caesarian. Never healed
right. Jagged edges. Butcher job. Alas, that's the package. For
sale: woman; twenty-years-married; used, but in good condition.
Everybody lies in the personals. Awkward process. Artificial. It's
so much easier when you're young. No encumbrances. No sad
stories to tell. Just something that happens. That feels right. Oh,
Adam! We started well. We did. You taught me to fly-fish. Standing
by me in the stream all day. Not the place I expected to fall in love.
But we did. Your gentle voice. And how you curved your arm over
mine, showing me the cast. I couldn't resist you. I shouldn't have.
And the air so clear. Not like this. Sticks to your skin up here.
Where? Maine. That's right, we're up in Maine.*

The sky, she saw, was close-in, a placid monochrome. Low clouds or a fog, lifting. *Day two.* For the next six, time would dilate. For once they would have too much of it.

Unfurling, she rolled off her side toward the middle of the bed. Probing his half, she found it empty; scanning the room, she saw no sign of him. She frankly admired this facet of Adam's physicality: an economy of movement that permitted him to rise without disturbing her. His kinetics had always been precise. Not so their son, whose body seemed a burden to his being, an unwieldy appendage. David would always be waking his lovers in the morning. Oh, well.

Pushing the sheets back, she righted herself and bounded out of bed, landing on both feet. At camp a bunkmate had once dubbed her "Hopper," alluding to this technique. She had preserved it, knowingly, as a habit, ever since; for her it had become a kind of keepsake, an artifact of her girlhood no less precious than an album or a ring. On some days it constituted her sole exertion, a rallying cry against middle age.

Their quarters were sparingly furnished—a Quaker dressing table, a lone arm chair, a modest hearth—enforcing an assumption of conviviality, the expectation that one was to spend most of one's time in the common areas. A raft of silver-framed photographs stood on the mantel: the Bents, or Kents. The realtor had disclosed little about them except that they had three grown children, lived outside Philadelphia, and didn't venture north until mid-July. Gazing at their faces under glass, Marion remarked the perverse intimacy of renting: how it provided access to a sanctum, the inner orbit of people's lives. Interspersed among the other visages she found one that interested her the most: the wife. She was eager to assemble a conception of their absent hostess, to correlate the décor with the decorator. She picked up frame containing the largest image—a casual pose, taken on a foredeck—and studied it. Her counterpart was a buxom, broad-shouldered woman—in her fifties here—with high cheekbones and open features; softly smiling, her mien was kindly and serene. She wore this expression often, Marion imagined: while watching the grandchildren at play, while listening to the chatter at the dinner table, and during all those signal moments when she felt the full impress of life's blessings. Perpetually offering approval to a world perpetually seeking it, such women form the good earth out of which completed souls grow.

Tears welled in her eyes. *Damn you, mother,* she thought, *why couldn't you be more like her?* Julia Scott, nee Phillips, had inherited from her father the same effete and cautious manner that had been passed on to him by his father, and which, it was said, could be traced two generations further back up the line to the figure of Harold A. Phillips, founder of the Midland Trust Company and author of the family fortune. Had she been a man, and had the family's controlling interest not been bought out, Marion's mother doubtlessly would have followed in the path of her ancestors, plying some narrow aspect of the banking trade from a corner office overlooking LaSalle Street; instead she had studied art history and subsequently obtained work as an assistant curator at the Art Institute. Matthew Scott, an ex-college-athlete in search of a career, had drifted into her life just as she had begun to fear spinsterhood. Her marriage to him had been a calculated risk; she had presumed she would be able to sculpt away the bumptious elements in his personality, tame him en route. But Marion's father had proven crasser, and his faults more enduring than her mother had estimated. The result was that it was she who was transformed by the marriage: the more frustration set in—the more apparent it became that she should have waited for her true knight—the more venomous she became, yet another suburban harridan.

Had she repeated the cycle? Marion wondered. There could be no excuse. From early on she had tried to reverse the pattern. Sarah and David were to have it better; they were to have constancy, a ready font of maternal warmth. But in Sarah's personality she had discerned the imprint of some inimical force. The girl held something back—a smile, a paragraph, some necessary emphasis—from every interaction, as though doubting that the other party would embrace the full scope of her being; even the way she moved, with balky, tentative strides, seemed tainted, the apologetic gait of a child attempting to remain unnoticed. Yet if Sarah had been damaged, the source of her injuries remained conjectural. She and Adam had never been screamers, either at the children or each other; and in effecting discipline, their approach had been an enlightened one, a studied matrix of rewards only thinly laced with punishments. Still, the inference was unshakeable: There had to have been a hitch, a bollixing of strands, in the weave of her motherhood. And if David's offhandedness, his worrisome insouciance, betrayed it less, this was only to be ascribed to his greater resilience, a suppler style of adaptation: the male character.

To arrest these ruminations she chose a shock to the senses. Abruptly, she pulled her nightgown over her head. In the chill air her nipples contracted; her skin tensed. At this latitude, she estimated, it was ten degrees colder than at home; June here reprised April in Quidnunquit. The atmosphere seemed liquid, pressing in on her with palpable heft; within it she felt suspended, a specimen immured in preservative. Detached and suddenly capable of objectivity, she turned to view herself in the antique standing mirror next to the closet. What she beheld, alas, was a mere commodity. There had to be millions of women in the world who approximated this look: shoulder-length tresses—not a touch of gray in them yet, but soon, perhaps, soon; size eight, hourglass figure—hopefully a six again, with dieting; B-cup breasts with lollipop-sized areolas—enough, but just barely. Just a generic Anglo-Saxon bride. Stock item. New ones minted every day.

"There you are."

"Was I among the missing?" Adam had settled into a deep fauteuil at the northeast corner of the living room. The morning light lay mostly at his back.

"You don't usually slip away like that."

It had not occurred to her, he supposed, that this was how it would have to begin. Their separation would entail a peeling away of ritual, a forsaking of routine; as each layer was shed there would be a fresh sense of loss. "I thought you might be sleeping late," he explained.

The room was without counter-lighting. As they spoke he remained an animate silhouette, an abstraction of himself. "I'm not sure that's a good idea," she said. "It might become a habit."
"I doubt it. You have too much self-discipline."
She relished this appraisal. More than anyone else, he was the person most qualified to gauge her character, her ability to start over. Divorcees fell into two camps, she believed: the energized and the enervated. Some women seemed to come alive, regaining a lost vitality, their native esprit; others languished, unable to rebirth themselves. If they did break up, she would confront the task of building a new life for herself, initially alone and unassisted. "I detest sloth," she confessed.
"A week of it won't hurt us."
"Promise?"
"There will be plenty to do when we get back."
His remark reverberated darkly, ambiguously. Back in Massachusetts, fortified or convinced by this interlude, would one of them make THE CALL? Divorce, as much as death, defies anticipation; we prepare for it, but we are never ready when it comes.
"Very well," she declared, taking up a stagey tone, "for the week, I shall do exactly as I please."
"Bravo! Let's be ourselves for once."
Unceremoniously, Marion flopped onto the large, spring-weary couch on her side of the room, letting her arms flail. Sighing, she tossed her head back and looked up, disinterestedly, at the ceiling, towards an instructive otherness outside herself. "God, Adam," she wondered, "how many masks have we held up to each other?"
Her metaphor pierced, tapping into a locule of self-awareness which, like an unrelieved abscess, had been festering for years. Rarely had he achieved authenticity in his relationships. An assortment of personas had been enlisted to stand in for him, shroud his vulnerable, meager self. "Too many," he admitted.
"Do other couples do that?"
"It depends, I think. If you've experienced previous cohabitations you've probably learned that it doesn't work."
"We never had that advantage."

"We never got to practice for each other."

"I should have met you later."

"By that point, sweetie, someone else would have snatched you up. You were always the marrying kind."

Without a doubt, a potent dynamic of endearment had affected all those who had romanced Marion. Before meeting Adam she had received three proposals. A succession of prematurely earnest, wide-eyed boys had perceived in her—in her demure smile and precious, Old World manner—the qualities of wifeliness. Ridiculous offers of marriage, politely deflected, had escaped their lips with the urgency of instinct. From the beginning, also, Adam had felt the same pull: an aroma about her, a fragrance carried in the aromatic arc at the base of her neck, the mixed scents of nap and perfume and cosseted flesh, had evoked memories of his mother, of the complex and soothing essence he had once been free to inhale, as a child in her arms.

"I'm afraid so," she accepted. "All my beaus were in a rush to present me to their families."

Images of a December weekend flooded in. He had chosen the beginning of the winter recess, a point less than six months into their romance, to introduce her to his parents. Just after their arrival an ice storm had struck, glassing in the Connecticut coast. For three days the four of them, held captive by glazed roads and downed limbs, had inhabited a crystalline landscape. Within that span she had easily won their hearts; they had reckoned her as compensation for the blighted fetus, confirmed by ultrasound to be a girl, lost when Adam was not yet walking. "I resisted you as long as I could," he said, "which, as it turned out, was not that long."

Five months, it was. Their courtship had begun in July and migrated steadily eastward. After Aspen he had visited her in Chicago, sheepishly wooing her at the family manse; then there were hotel room trysts in Detroit and Niagara; subsequently a series of visits to the Princeton campus; finally a weekend in Manhattan. Priming her with sonnets and a rose, he had proposed to her in the park as they sat huddled against the November chill. She had accepted with a smile, a nod, and a distinctly uttered, "Yes," maintaining a calm, an assuredness, which perplexed him. Later she would explain that she had rehearsed this answer many times: from the beginning, she had known he was the one.

"It seemed like forever, as I recall."

"I didn't want my folks to scold us for being rash; I didn't want you to start off on the wrong foot with them."

"Your parents have always been good to me, Adam."

"Of course; they adore you." Whenever he made this admission, it was partly with envy. On his own, he had never been able to achieve a clean linkage with his father; their conversations had always been stilted, impeded by a glandular static, an Oedipal subtext. In Marion's presence, however, they were more able to be at ease with each other; her warbling small talk opened up a channel, a rhythm, they could not find by themselves.

"And I adore them."

He knew that his parents wouldn't shun her after they divorced; they were bigger than that. Yet Marion's mother, upon learning of their split, would swiftly delete him from her address book; later, in consoling her daughter, she would soberly—didactically—enumerate his faults and praise her for finally opting out. "I wasn't quite as big a hit with your family," he lamented, letting his arms tumble off the arm rests.

"With my mother, you mean."

"Mostly."

"You got along fine with my father."

"I did," he reflected. "We had some good times together." His reminiscences of his father-in-law—"Matt," as he gruffly called himself—largely comprised outdoor scenes, triumphal moments from pheasant shoots, fishing expeditions, and climbing sorties. In Matt's company he had felt redblooded, audacious, abundantly male. "I enjoyed your father's company," he added.

"He and my mother were an odd combination. He should have married someone like Aunt Jean."

Matt's brother, Amos, the uncle who had provided the set for their initial days together, had hewn to the path of likeness in choosing a mate. No less rambunctious and ill-suited to city life than his brother, he had paired with a coequal, a brawny and energetic girl, scornful of fineries. Jean had shared his restlessness, his appetite for open space. Though both were from the East, they had ventured west after school, first to ski, then to take up the ranching trade.

"They say that opposites attract."

"There's no single formula."

On a scale of polarities, the Falks would have fallen into the intermediate range. In the aggregate, they were neither similar nor dissimilar; a haphazard meshwork of complementarities constituted their bond. Yet, with the years, the weave of this had worn thin; stretched, slackened, and frayed, it would next commence to disintegrate. Now they must either darn or discard.

"You and I..." Adam faltered, ruing his choice of tense, "just seemed to go together."

"Like peas and carrots."

"People used to think we were brother and sister."

Once they had prided themselves on eliciting this perception. Their physiognomies had overlapped as much, or more, than most siblings, and their complexions had moved seasonally through the same modest range of tones. But time, inevitably, had exposed their genetics: on his bad days he looked puffy and sallow; she, on hers, pallid and parchment-skinned. His coding was mesomorphic; hers ectomorphic. By old age they would form a study in contrasts. "I remember," she said, unable to suppress a slight, prideful smile. "I used to think we were predestined for each other."

Adam brought his hands up to his chin and laced them together. Frowning, he countered, "As it turns out, we never abdicated free will."

"Good morning! Did you sleep well?"

"We slept late, certainly." They had set nine o'clock as the time to have breakfast. Ordinarily they were both out the door by this hour, Adam to tend to his hospital cases, Marion to join a tennis group or a volunteer effort. "It feels decadent," Adam confessed.

Clarence was pouring coffee. The table was set with Wedgwood: indigo filigree over antique white. "You'll settle into it," he predicted. "It takes a couple of days to get your bearings up here."

"It's so peaceful," Marion mused, panning the horizon.

"That's what makes these islands special," the chef asserted. "They provide a type of quiet that's good for the soul."

"It's pretty quiet for us at home these days, also," Adam disclosed. "We're recently empty-nested."

"You're at an important time in your lives. It's a time when people reassess."

Served up so quickly, this comment struck them as nearly ready-made, concocted, almost, from foreknowledge.

"It's true," Marion heard herself say. Normally it would have been her instinct to dissimulate, to skirt the dim masses of angst that crowded her soul, yet now she felt strangely incapable of editing her remarks; some impetus compelled her to speak as one engaged in therapy, withholding nothing. "I don't really know where I'm going from here."

Widening momentarily, the old man's eyes seemed to turn opalescent, the unsettled colors of the day. "I'm sure this week will help you decide," he assured her. Then with Oriental grace he turned and withdrew to his work in the kitchen.

Adam detected a forlorn expression crossing his wife's face, a look he was used to seeing on the terminally ill, and on their kith and kin. Reflexively he touched his hand to her forearm, formulating words of comfort: "Your French is still excellent; you should think of doing something with it." At Sarah Lawrence, Marion had been a Romance language major, *français plus que l'italien,* but after graduation her facility with the Gallic tongue had served as little more than an adornment to her social patter, an aid in the decipherment of café menus; she had always blankly rejected any suggestion that she might teach or ply her linguistic skills within the travel industry.

"I'm so mixed up, Adam," she continued, oblivious to his comment. "About me. About us. About everything." Searching for distraction, she turned her gaze outward, through the porch screen. Not far from the house a lone gull hovered in the overcast sky. Enough of a breeze was moving to allow the bird to maintain its position; neither advancing nor falling back, it hung complacently on the wind. *Like that,* she told herself. *That's how you make it through this. Don't fight it. Just float. See what comes. This husband or a new one: what will be, will be.*

"Let's just have a quiet day," he said, turning to a new tack. "I think I'll work on a jigsaw puzzle."

"That sounds tame enough. I haven't noticed; do they have any here?"

"There are always puzzles in places like this, dearest. People who don't read have to have something to do on rainy days."

Assimilating a yawn, Marion lifted her hands over her head and then, unclasping them, let them arch down to her sides. A wing beat. Beneath her close-woven top, her breasts, pert orbs suspended in a caramel field, swelled and parted invitingly. *My dove, my pretty one. How fine you are, still.* "Well, if you're going to do that, I guess I'll—"

"Snoop?"

"Adam!"

"I'm not blaming you; it's only natural to be curious. If I didn't have you to do the legwork, I'm sure I'd be at it myself. Let me know if you turn up anything interesting."

Marion yielded him the point, setting aside any protest. Truthfully, his perceptiveness flattered her. If to date is to house-hunt, then to be married is to own. In matrimony we live within each other, discovering the hissing pipes, the drafty corners, the creaking floorboards that are revealed only after occupancy. Her habit of picking through the personal effects of other people was one of her more obscure flaws, a rattling pane in an attic window; as a husband he had taken in all of her flaws, probed every recess. "From what I've seen so far," she conceded, "they seem quite ordinary."

"Ordinary people don't own islands."

"What I meant was—"

"HERE we are!" Clarence bustled back onto the porch carrying, on his lacquered serving tray, the morning repast: strawberries and

Cream of Wheat for him, a soft-boiled egg for her. And once he had served these items, he returned, as on the day before, with a basket containing slices from a simple, seedless loaf. To their relief, when they tasted the bread, they found it lighter and more palatable. Nothing savory but a better effort: more freshly baked and made, perhaps, from different dough.

"I can't believe we ever bought into this stuff."

After breakfast they had returned to the living room. Outside, a desultory light rain had begun. Marion sat pressed into one end of the couch, her feet tucked demurely beneath her haunches, skimming a yellowing issue of *Vogue.* Behind her Adam sat hunched over a card table; from a game closet in the pantry he had selected a puzzle bearing the image of the painting, "Shipping in Down East Waters," by Fitz Hugh Lane.

"What stuff?"

Staring down at a model in evening wear emerging from a limousine, Marion imagined a range of captions: "What Every Girl Wants: A Diamond by _____;" "A Dress by _____;" "A Private Banking Relationship with _____."

"This stuff!" she exclaimed, waving the page at him. "Madison Avenue! Glitter! We've all been conditioned to want it, to think that we're lacking without it."

"That's consumerism, sweetie."

"God, what a lie!" she protested. "I've had enough of it!"

In his hand, Adam held part of a bowsprit. On the box top he had counted two brigs and a schooner. *Can't place this one yet.* "I'm not sure you can get away from it," he observed blandly, taking up a new piece.

"No, but I can resist. I can stop trying to be Peg."

By unspoken consensus, Peg Sherman was the reigning queen of the fifty-odd households that comprised the Chafee Point Neighborhood Association. Bounded on three sides by the Bay and partly, on the fourth, by a salt marsh, the Association's sense of identity, of forming a discrete social tableau, rested as much on its demographics as on its geography. To move inland from the Point was to descend a gradient of prosperity; along the wrack-strewn coves which bordered it, and more so, away from the water altogether, the properties became starkly less affluent. Being a "Pointer" thus entailed the acceptance of a certain conspicuousness about one's wealth; for some a corollary was that they forsook all modesty in displaying it. No one typified this arrogance, this hubris, more than Peg. Ever since marrying Ronald, a brashly successful alarm-systems entrepreneur, she had devoted every effort to submerge the fact that her maiden name ended in a vowel—egad!—and that she had been raised in humble circumstances in East Providence. Peg threw lavish parties, chaired social committees, and presided over galas: whatever served to grab linage in the society pages. Near the peak of her powers now, she seemed to levitate above the rest of the Quidnunquit trophy-wives, their garish idol.

"But you can't be her, dear; you're old money." It was still possible to flatter her with this trope. A conceit they both shared, one of the more unbecoming aspects of their linkage, was the notion that they were both well-born, bred to understand the virtues of restraint.

"No," Marion reflected, "but she rubs off on you. She makes you want to compete with her."

"Competitive pearls?"

"It's gold, in her case. She owns more carats than any girl I know."

"Perhaps she grows them in a garden."

"On a farm, I should say."

Bangles and beads. Among women, Adam had learned, jewelry constituted a form of semaphore, an invidious private language. Among themselves they kept score in a code of spangles. "You're right," he said. "She clanks when she moves."

"That's Peg." In the ironic and philosophical section of her mind, Marion held the figure of her neighbor up for examination, considering her not as an individual, but as a type: the Cleopatra next door. Women everywhere scratch and claw for this, she thought: to be one perch above. And for what? For a bliss drawn from comparisons. "I'm going to start a counter movement," she announced.

"Hmmm?"

"I'm go to go shabby. Old clothes, holes in the sleeves—the works."

"People will say you're on drugs."

"Let them." Within her a moral upwelling—a righting reflex—was taking hold. She felt dawningly capable of casting off ill-considered habits, baked-in assumptions. "I'm tired of the hypocrisy," she declared. "I think we should have the Caffertys over for dinner."

The Caffertys were part of the plucky human infrastructure of Quidnunquit—of any town. Madge was a hairdresser and Joe was a carpenter. Both spoke in the demotic, the gruff, syncopated accent of blue-collar New England; both routinely perpetrated atrocities on the King's English. Yet what they lacked in gentility they recouped in earnestness, in decency, in uprightness. The Falks knew of no two people who were more trustworthy or unselfish; their integrity was absolute.

"*That* will cause a stir."

Curious, now, to read his reaction to her rant, she craned to see him over the back of the couch. On his face she observed an expression that was wry and sardonic, yet tentatively approving. Inwardly she felt a thaw, the flow of some vital principal across a dark edge. Expatiating, she continued, "Can't you just picture it? We'll invite the biggest snobs we know, the Ward-Smiths and the Truslows."

Quizzically, he grasped the "We" in her presentation. Was she merely being hypothetical? Stoically he played along. "We'll be off the Ward-Smith's 'A' list by dessert," he predicted.

"Good riddance! Christ, Adam, they're such fakes! Why have we tolerated them all this time?"

Her rhetoric struck a chord. These were the kind of people who wore their pedigrees on their sleeves; the Ward-Smiths, they reminded you, had been big in textiles, the Truslows in packaging. Self-appointed, self-important defenders of the Old Guard, they took it upon themselves to administer a sniff test to all new arrivals on the Point. Those who passed were placed on the "in" roster and presented around; those who didn't were left to languish, suffer a slow social asphyxia. "You're right," he said, advancing the theme. "I've always felt we had to put up with them—as part of the process."

"What process?"

"You know: genuflect before them, collect a pass, get invited to one of their parties; bend a knee for some other asshole and his wife, collect another token, get invited to their party; and so on."

"That's a cute little synopsis of things."

"You like it? Perhaps I'll send it into the local rag."

"You can title it, 'From the Anals of Quidnunquit.'"

Adam emitted a chuffing sound, an expulsive little laugh. "I'll share the byline with you," he promised.

"Darling, you're too kind." And then, as though toppled by the force of something moving off-center within her, the Newtonian physics of spiritual realignment, Marion sprawled sideways onto the middle of the couch; her unbound hair formed auburn swirls on the faded chintz. "I just want to run away," she announced, or pleaded, gazing off into empty space.

Ever so slightly, it seemed to Adam, an unseen giant hand was turning the rim of the kaleidoscope through which he viewed and understood his life. A new configuration was appearing, refulgent in his imagination. He knew of several couples who, at a comparable stage, had become partners in wanderlust; having reached a point of inflection into diminishing responsibility, a vista from which old age and death could be seen gathering on the horizon, they had claimed sanction to roam. In some cases the movement was geographic; in others, existential. The Sylvesters had bought a cattle ranch and moved to Montana; the Kramers had given up legal and accounting practices to open a gallery; the Whitmans had simply "dropped out." But regardless of the particulars, those who had turned off the beaten path rarely came back. In their new incarnations they seemed to catch hold of something—a still water current—that pulled them on. "I'll join you," he said.

"You will?"

"Damned right. Respectability, routine—I've had enough of it."

An earnest admission, she wondered, or a ploy? People often made crazy, desperate admissions to fend off a split. "What would you do?" she explored.

Adam tumbled a puzzle piece between thumb and forefinger. "I don't know. I'd like to travel but still feel useful."

"You could work for the Peace Corps or the Red Cross."

"Sorry, sweetie: Mosquito netting, war zones—that's where I draw the line."

"What then?"

"I could be a hotel doctor on an island somewhere. Tend to hangovers and the occasional grippe, otherwise work on my golf game. And how about you? Where would you wander off to?"

Marion turned onto her back and cupped her hands behind her head: a daydreamer's pose. She felt approximately thirteen, once more able to believe in picture book adventures. "Oh, some place quiet. I'd find a chalet in the mountains."

In the dust-speckled air between them, Adam intercepted his wife's vision, beheld it exactly. "In the Alps?" he confirmed.

"Oui, ça serait tres joli."

They were in it together now, a Helvetian diorama. Alternately, they added embellishments.

"We could live above a little village."

"And ski down for lunch, in season."

"In the summer we can tour the lowlands."

"Provence, Tuscany."

"That sounds like a lovely plan."

Adam snapped a piece into place. "I think so, too."

June 22nd
Matthew Island, Maine

Dear Judy—

I don't really know why I'm penning you this note, since there's no mail service up here, and I surely will have had coffee with you before it arrives. I guess it's just a matter of habit: I always write my number-one girlfriend when I'm off on vacation.

So far, this week is turning out better than I expected. We're on a teensy island way out in the mouth of the bay.

(Actually, I'm not sure where the bay ends and the ocean begins, but we're somewhere near the transition.) Just to get here we had to make a seven- or eight-mile passage out from Mount Desert Isle in a little runabout. The waves were high, and I got soaked! It's a place worth coming to, though. The sea is all around you. I love its taste and smell. I feel like I'm on a cruise ship that's been decked out with trees and shrubs.

As you PROBABLY KNOW, we're being catered to by this crusty old chef who's a retired teacher. As a second career, I gather, he cooks for well-heeled types in places like this. SOMEONE *(I know it's you, but I haven't yet figured out how you set this up!)* commissioned him to prepare our food for a week. He's quite droll—a little dry-roasted peanut of a man—but he's entirely up to the task. We've had some fine meals already, especially breakfast, which seems to be his forte.

Truthfully, I don't know what's going to happen to Adam and me. I thought I was coming up here to begin saying goodbye to him, and I know he expected as much. We're being very honest about where things stand, and it's been refreshing. We even started to relax with each other: I can't remember how long it's been since it was that way. This morning we were actually joking about running away together—joking, mind you. I know that you would say that you can't beat a dead horse, but this one is still breathing, barely.

Enough for now. I'm off to summon a veterinarian.

> Abundant hugs,
> Marion

On the throne again. Seat of wisdom. Afternoon shift; afternoon shit. Digestion not as regular now. Used to be a once-a-day man. First thing in the morning, like clockwork. That's *what happens as you go along: The timing slips. Women have it worse, for sure. Their red friend. Double trouble.*

Does something funny to your thinking, this. Such a welter of daydreams. I wonder if anybody's researched the topic. "Cognitive Changes During Defecation." Appearing in next month's Journal of Psychogastroenterology. *Supported by a grant from the Julia and Matthew Scott Foundation. Not so far-fetched really. They probably would have lent a hand if I'd gone back for a Ph.D. Research, I'm sure, would have suited me better. Was never really right for the wards. Guaranteed respectability the main appeal. Not so much, these days. Healing's become bourgeois. If I'd had more chutzpah, I'd have gone into business. But I wanted something safe. Coward. Now I have it. Orifices and innards: that's my bailiwick. No limelight there.*

I'd like to keep you, Marion, truly I would. We fell apart so slowly, I hardly noticed. Ironic really: I'm trained to monitor. Heart disease, heartache: they both creep up on you.

Just a little more time, please. If you could give me that, I would show you changes. Weight loss would be easy—I used to wrestle, remember? And I really will learn to dance. I'll even make the bed. And I'll chuck it all if you really want to disengage. I'd be a bum or an expat for you. I would.

Done. Can't believe they buy such cheap tissue. Big money and they won't shell out for a soft wipe. Ah! That stings! Skinflints! Have to leave a note in the guestbook: Enjoyed everything except your choice of T.P. Recommend you go more upscale. *One more and that should do it. Yes: finished. Arise, flush, and go forth. Make amends.*

"Is it time for a little nip?"

Adam had been studying a field guide, *Trees of North America.* Setting it down, he glanced at the position of the sun, which, as had been the case all day, appeared as a creamy lozenge lurking behind veils of mist and cloud. "Why not?" he said.

Drinking was something the Falks had learned to do well together. The curriculum of prior experience, all the chagrin-filled mornings and extirpated memories, had taught them to pace themselves. Now, when with company, they stopped short of overdoing it; and if it was only the two of them, they got blurry at the same rate. Just as importantly, they were amicable under the influence. Adam became loquacious, a voluble raconteur; Marion, by degrees, became giddy, then goofy, a comedic distortion of herself. Indeed, if by the clear light of day they struggled to maintain this jocularity, it was one of the more hopeful failings of their marriage: alcohol induced in them a falsetto which, though ephemeral, pointed to a companionability still within their reach.

"Make mine a double," Marion added, in afterthought. "I feel like getting a little stewed."

"I promise not to tell."

"I have a theory," she called after him as he rose and approached the liquor cabinet.

"Let's hear it."

"I think we're given two lives to lead, one after the other. Until we're forty, we do what we have to do to push back the jungle: we grow, mate, procreate, learn to feed ourselves, and raise our young until they can repeat the cycle. It's all biological determinism. After that we get a second chance; we're free to redefine ourselves. But by that point most people have done enough stupid things to ruin it for themselves; they're too busy feeling tired or wounded or inadequate to take up the challenge."

Adam cinched his fingers around the neck of a Dewar's bottle, now an impromptu talisman. Tersely, he asked, "Is that what we've done, ruin it?"

In the gray, unflattering light she beheld him: her husband. This hesitating and tender man with whom she had cast her lot, chosen to stroll the planet. He had his mother's eyes, an unassuming shade of olive, lightly brown-spindled. The rest of his features—the high forehead, the Donatello nose, the incisor-rich smile—were his father's; patrilineally, he had inherited a countenance which made him seem more unapproachable, less vulnerable than he was. "I guess that's what we're here to find out," she conceded.

Adam finished pouring. "For my part, it wasn't deliberate," he said. "Ice?" he asked.

"I'll take it neat. Please, just come back."

Such a simple request, he thought, and so gladdening; he had grown accustomed to being held at a distance. Obligingly, he returned with their drinks and sat down next to her.

"You'll be completely honest with me?" Marion asked. Her gaze was limpid and unwavering—no less mesmerizing, it struck him, than on that sultry day in May twenty-one years ago, when they had exchanged vows.

"Certainly."

"I have to have that now."

"I know."

She took a draught: liquid courage. Cupping her hands prayerfully around her glass, she asked, "Has there been anyone else?"

Adam felt an incongruous puerile pride well within him. Like a brown-nosing schoolboy, he would get credit for answering this correctly. "No," he said.

For the follow-up Marion bowed her head. "How close have you come?"

How close? *Horseshoes and hand grenades. Adultery too?* His conscience highlighted a pair of near misses. The more innocuous of the two was the time Nina Petterutti had made her sad little attempt to seduce him. Stopping by on a day when Marion had chosen to linger at the beach, she had found him alone; while prattling about child-rearing issues she had maneuvered close to him and, implying comparable treatment for his more sensate appendages, begun to massage his big toe. Refusing her had been as much a matter of aesthetics as will power: she was a big, sloppy woman afflicted with eczema and overburdened by life—not his type. More tantalizing, by far, had been his encounter with Mickey Lewis. (Such a funny nickname for such an attractive woman; he had never learned the real one.) At a fundraiser in Hull they had found themselves compressed into a corner. A willful, nervous redhead feeling lonely inside her marriage, she had embraced him as a confidant, offered up a litany of doubts; reciprocally, he had wooed her with sympathetic listening, an attitude of fatherly compassion. Impossibly, within the space of half an hour, they had transgressed: mentally, they had fucked. "I've had to decline two or three invitations," he admitted.

"Should I ask whom they were from?"

"No one you're close to." He was relieved to be able to employ the present tense. Nina, the large woman, had grown obese and obsessively self-pitying; after their children's paths had diverged Marion had mercifully allowed the relationship to ebb. "Your friends are blameless."

"That's nice to know. I like my friends."

"I can give you names—"

"It's not necessary. All men flirt. I just need to know that nothing ever happened."

"Nothing did. I swear."

They had had this conversation before, whole and in parts. Previously, though, his reassurances had only carried the weight of ritual, a refrain all wives solicit from their husbands, dissembling or not. Yet these words, this pledge, loomed larger. They had the heft of truth. "Thank you for that," she said.

"You don't have to, sweetie. I was just holding up my end of the bargain."

So: he wasn't a cheater. She had never really suspected otherwise. He had hardly had reason. Sex once or twice a week—until recently, at least; hot-cooked meals at night; a well-feathered nest: She had furnished all the basics. She liked to think, also, that she had cast a spell over him, bound him to fidelity with a web of irresistible charms—the cozy feline timbre of her voice, her skin's pampered softness, the potent blend of pheromones that wafted through her pores—and that her power to hold him in the marital seine, if she chose to wield it, remained undiminished. Vainly, she balked at the idea of releasing him. "If you hadn't," she admitted, "I'm not sure I could have gotten over it."

"I wouldn't have expected you to." Musingly, Adam swirled his drink and took a sip. The pithiness of the scotch seemed apposite to the theme of their conversation. "Is it my turn now?"

Marion nodded, setting her weight back in the cushions.

"How about you then? Have you done any shopping around?"

"That's a bald way to put it."

"Sorry, is there a preferred euphemism for adultery?"

"I like *straying*."

"All right, have you strayed?"

"No, darling, I have not."

"Not even with Kent Olsen?" She could scarcely blame him for this bit of skepticism. Kent was Quidnunquit's very own Lothario. Salon owner, winter surfer, and rakish parvenu, he had probably bedded half the women in town; to be among the number who had copulated with him had become almost trite. "I thought everybody had."

"He offered to make me a member of his 'circle,' as he puts it."

"Or to make you, with his member."

"Yes, but I passed."

"Why?"

Why? That was the corollary question, wasn't it? One's reasons mattered. Fidelity came in different stripes.

"It wouldn't have been fair."

The word left a trace, a clarifying afterimage, in each of their minds. Every contest must have its rules, for, as even young children know, without strictures, without some delimitation of the options, there can be no significance, no reward, in the outcome. Now it seemed possible that they had held onto this—fairness, an architecture of decency—in the conduct of their marriage. Granted, they had been rancorous, intransigent, and at times, vindictive; but so, too, do athletes jostle and elbow. In the end, though, they had respected the lines; they not committed any game fouls. And therein was the hope that was left to them.

Adam peered out across the Bay toward the northern horizon, toward New Brunswick and Nova Scotia, toward lands they had not traveled. Wistfully, he imagined that someday they might still see them, the great timbered expanses beyond the border, above America. "I agree," he said.

"Are you enjoying it here, so far?"

This inquiry, posed as they were savoring their last spoonfuls of caramelized custard, came unexpectedly. Throughout dinner, Clarence had barely spoken.

"We're never had an island to ourselves before," Adam managed. "It's certainly a new experience."

"It's growing on us," Marion added.

The old chef's features lifted into an expression which seemed to connote approval, as if they had responded in the way that was expected of them to a test, some undisclosed appraisal. "That it does," he said. "To spend time here is to be engaged in a process. One day follows another, but the days are not the same. Tomorrow you will feel fully at ease, disconnected from the pace of things; by Thursday you will feel yourselves reviving, gaining energy. There is a sequence."

This tone—positivistic, serene, almost gnostic—was familiar. Marion strained the waters of memory for a cognate. Had it been at some palmy resort, that blithe, welcome-to-paradise attitude the greeters are paid to exude? No, no match there. Her mind then glossed to the scene of a campfire under tall trees. Oregon: That was it. Eight or ten years before, her father had invited them to raft down a wild section of the Rogue River.(Such had been his method of annealing his bonds with his children once they were grown; he would enlist them in excursions to remote and untamed places, curing grounds for the soul.) The trip had spanned five days, constituting a minor odyssey. Each night, their guide, a scraggly software engineer turned back-to-nature type, had made divinatory pronouncements concerning the experiences that awaited them downstream, foretelling not only the coming thrills, the thunderous rapids and vicious current-sinks they would encounter, but also certain modifications of perspective, in one's *Weltanschauung*, that were destined to occur.

Clarence, she saw, was of the same ilk. Now she had him figured. At a sufficient remove from the world, beyond the daily bustle, we all become romantics. We want to believe in renewal; we are eager to hear its stories. Thus in every far-off spot there are the narrators, those that articulate the fiction of a place. They tell us that we shall live longer, love better for having visited their retreat. They promise that we will regain the up slope. They are binders of spells, nature's minstrels. Harmless they are, if nothing else. Yet frequently they charm us by what they try to do. "I'm sure you're right," she said in a subdued voice. "We should have done this years ago."

The snow, as forecast, had started after midnight. In other seasons he would have had the comfort of that miscellany of noises which gives texture to the dark, but on that night, now relived as a dream, he had floundered in silence.

His consciousness, he had discovered, could become a void. Without stimulus, without the orienting drone of the occasional passing car or the responsive dog bark, without so much as the slap and sough of waves against the shore—the bay had been quiet that evening— his thoughts could not take seed. Had he been able to he would have reached for the alarm-radio, summoned a chorus off the airwaves, but the quiet in which he had lain had exerted a self-preserving force; it had interdicted movement, or any action that would disrupt its hold; he had become its prisoner, awaiting reprieve through sleep.

In the other instances when he had slept away from Marion— when he had attended medical conventions solo, or she had slipped off to catch up with a college friend—there had always been some audible nuisance, a snuffling child or the hubbub of a city to lend particularity to the unlit world. The necessity of having her by his side, of being entrained in the gentle commotion she created, had not previously occurred to him. But on that night he had been humbled to learn how much he needed her little sibilant expirations, her periodic quarter-rotations to secure his own rest. And by the morning after those insomniac hours, he had acquired an inchoate fear of sleeping alone.

This dauntingly silent night had transpired in January, five or six years before. Since then the same enslaving stillness had returned to him regularly, as a dream. Tonight, however, the stillness exhibited a different character; his dream seemed to hybridize and combine with a new one. Though he remained immobile, horizontally suspended in a mute vastness, there was movement within that which contained him, indigo currents flowing beneath the surface of the dark; inside stasis there was flux, undulant tides forming byways through the deep.

Presently, he was transported along a vein of the richest royal blue, a broad rip angling irresistibly through the depths. Its course ushered him lower and lower, further and further from the canopy of day, the spectacle of the world. Reaching a terminus, it pressed him onto a blank, flat surface, the floor of a phantasmal sea. Here there was neither sound nor light, only nullity, a vacancy of experience. Death, he judged—the surcease of every possibility—must abide in this place. He tried to struggle, to raise himself up, but a weight was on his head. Now there was no air to breathe, *no air...*

"Adam?"

The voice was distant and diffuse. A siren calling.

"Adam!"

This time it sounded human; someone come to help. The muscles of his throat constricted around an inaudible reply.

"Wake up, dear."

Hands fluttered around him, arranging. A chill on his back was curtailed, the pressure on his head relieved.

"You had the sheets off, and your head was under the pillow. You must have been having a nightmare."

"I guess I was. You rescued me."

"Go back to sleep. You can tell me about it in the morning."

"If I'm able to remember it," he murmured, "I will."

WEDNESDAY

The new day, still only a pale turquoise luminescence, a diffuse backlighting against the gauzy curtains, was slow to arrive. Awake too early, Marion lay in bed attempting to muster her thoughts for what had become a therapeutic exercise.

You were truly over somebody, a friend had once told her, when you could be happy that they had found a new love. She had never doubted the wisdom of this advice; it seemed as good a litmus test as any for determining the spoilage of a relationship. Offhandedly she would sometimes glimpse other women—silken blondes slinking down grocery aisles, luscious-lipped Jewesses palavering in dress boutiques—trying to construe them as successors, plausible renderings of the stepmother their children might someday have to endure. Yet inevitably these attempts at self-inoculation, these ad-lib modelings of Adam's future disintegrated too quickly; in the stream of experience she could not hold on to such apparitions long enough to see them in the round. A better venue for fingering the pulse of her marriage, she had discovered, was this half-alert, half-drowsing state of mind: Here, with painstaking stagecraft, she had constructed a dreamscape, a seraglio populous with all the women Adam had once, even briefly, seemed to favor; here, quite systematically, she matched him with friends' wives, curvaceous colleagues, dinner-party pals.

This morning, starring unknowingly, Lynn Weaver was playing the role of Adam's live-in, his soon-to-be second wife. A specter from his adolescence, briefly a girlfriend, she had tracked him down after hearing, through the hometown grapevine, that he was once again at liberty; she had left her own childless, failing marriage, and they had moved together into a high-ceilinged, recently refurbished garden apartment in the Back Bay. Lynn was an artist and a free spirit; she also ran marathons, endorsed macrobiotics, and practiced tai chi. For Adam she constituted the ideal conduit into a new life; with her Bohemian mores came a breezy, nonjudgmental mind-set which would allow him to redefine himself, achieve a better balance.

She pictured them now, at home in their urban nook, relaxing on a weekday evening: the cabernet warming in their palms, the marijuana fumes curling in the soffits, some ethereal music setting the mood. Seeing them legs-intertwined, languidly engaged in a prelude to foreplay, she tried to be glad for them; hearing the cozy interplay of their voices, his deft baritone punctuating her soft vibrato, she tried to conclude that it was for the best, this cool rechartering of lives. But again, as on many other mornings, her sensibilities detected something abhorrent in this scene, this casting. Adam—her Adam—did not belong in the arms of this New Age waif. BITCH! SLUT! her consciousness shouted. BE GONE! And with an imaginary marker, employing heavy, childlike strokes, she reached out and blackened the visage of the other woman. Still the only prospect to have succeeded in these auditions was herself.

The cats—that's what he missed most up here. Lounging on the settee at the end of the porch, waiting for Marion to finish her ablutions, Adam thought of Isis and Osiris, the two chocolate-point Siamese they had obtained two years before from a breeder in Weymouth, a rumpled but kindly widow who had pleaded with them to eschew declawing. She had made other requests—almost edicts—too: don't have them fixed; don't feed them table scraps; don't let them go outside. With adolescent obstinacy they had ignored every one; their pedigreed felines had been neutered, overfed, and loosed to the perils of the neighborhood, left to fend for themselves against a motley population of toms, opossums, skunks, and retrievers. From the beginning, though, these lithesome creatures had proven well adapted to life in the suburban wilds; rarely had they returned wounded from a night's prowl, and if so, it had only been with a few minor scratches, testaments to a mere territorial skirmish.

They would have been quite at home on this island, Adam mused. He pictured them gamboling over the rocks, pussy-footing around tidal pools, pawing through aggregations of clams and wrack. Pets too, he supposed, could be refreshed by a change of scene—why had they not brought them? Their company would have been at least as pleasant as any pair of humans. From an American Lit class, still ensconced in his memory, he retrieved the lines from Whitman:

> ...I could turn and live with the animals, they are so placid
> and self-contained...
> They do not sweat and whine about their condition...
> Not one is dissatisfied, not one is demented with the mania
> of owning things...

These particular cats, moreover, had a lesson to teach. They did for each other—a full repertoire of hind-grooming—what they could not do for themselves. Was it because they were litter-mates? The question seemed moot. To Adam, this morning, the message seemed particularly clear: we live better reciprocally; we live better as two than one.

If palms can be read, she reasoned, then why not, also, faces? Not the eyes, those arresting portals through which, perhaps all too directly, we view the soul; and not the mouth, that valvèd spout which, audibly or not, expresses all our elations, sorrows, and misgivings: just the more immobile tissue, the fleshy mask which surrounds them. In the worried skin that spans the forehead and rims the orbits, in its creases and crow marks, is there not also inscribed a code comparable to the telltale lines of the hand? Considering this question, Marion paused before the bathroom mirror and delayed the application of an emollient.

What method to employ? In deciphering a visage, should one take each line, in its unique length and shape, as the confirmation of a particular trait, a specific virtue or shortcoming, or gather all into a larger sum, a gestalt? Briefly she attempted the latter, more complicated feat, trying to behold her lineaments in the aggregate, to perceive a hieroglyphic, a character: nothing came of this. She decided, then, that the trick must lie in singling out the most distinctive lines for study. The wrinkles in her brow, though still immature, impressed as generic; she doubted their power to carry portents. No, there could only be predictiveness in the more variant markings, in the final, capricious, embellishing strokes of the Demiurge.

Here: this slim little dash, a tiny scar, low on her brow. Aslant over her eye, it resembled a stress symbol, an *accent aigu.* She imagined it to be the signature of a latent spiritedness, a joie de vivre she had yet to step into. And here: these symmetrical, vertical arcs at the corners of her mouth. They seemed parentheses embracing an expansible text. Her face, she saw, was emphatically punctuated, confidently authored. It was configured for zest and merriment, a heartiness of experience. It was not a face suited to an embittered divorcee, a vanquished soul. A happy and unforeseen destiny was written upon it.

Very well, she thought, observing the mechanics of her own unfolding grin, *let's bring it on.*

The legends of Arthur tell of a realm—by some accounts an island, by others an isthmus—that lay between Land's End and the Isles of Scilly. It was a halcyon region, abundant with fruit and overflowing with game. Here, it was said, Arthur and his knights would come to replenish themselves after campaigns of war. In its fair clime their wounds quickly healed, and their spirits were refreshed. A

*royal haven at the tip of Cornwall, this place came to be
known as "Lyonnesse."*

*Welcome, guests. We hope that you enjoy your time on
this island—our island. For us it is another Lyonnesse. We
have been renewed and fortified by the days spent here,
entranced by the rhythms of wind and waves. May it be so
for you as well. THE BENTS*

"Adam?"

"Yes?"

"Have you seen the guest book?"

"I can't say I have."

Marion hesitated for a beat, a caesura, as if considering alternative paths through the conversation. "There's an inscription in it by the owners; they sound like romantics."

He had always had an aversion to guest books: all those saccharine one-liners. Someday he would pen something blasphemous into someone's carefully kept register: *Such a drab little place...wouldn't stay an extra day if you paid me...can't wait to get back to modern plumbing...* "What have you learned about them so far?" he asked.

Unbending, she left off her inspection of the log, migrating away from the antique side table where it was kept; she had been circling the living room for a while, examining each artifact, every keepsake, with the obsessive thoroughness of a professional bidder. "Oh, they're older; they have grandchildren." Wistfully, her imagination transported her to a sun-splashed summer lawn thickly bordered with azaleas and rhododendrons; a brood of cherubic preschoolers frolicked around her, playing at some just-invented game. "They're where we would be in about ten years."

Again, he apprehended the ambiguity in her syntax: neither *will be* nor *would have been.* On the subject of their future she was becoming, if not encouraging, at least open-ended. "I'm not sure I'm ready for the next generation of Falks," he confessed. "Aren't we still raising this one?"

74

Marion stopped at the hearth and sat down on the upholstered bench in front of it, her back to the fireplace. Gazing across a painterly distance at her husband, she was struck by one simple and impudent truth: divorce was unnatural, a thing perverse. Though she might detach herself from Adam, dwell separately, even take up with another man, she would always be his mate. Together, out of the broth of their loins, they had conjured new beings; afoot in their children, their linkage had been sealed. "We can add a few finishing touches," she conceded, "if they'll listen."

"I worry more about David."

"I do, too. He's so casual about things."

Out of the many affecting memories from his son's Little League years, Adam retrieved a cameo scene. Bed-checking on a night when a friend was sleeping over, he had discovered David's long-limbed form dangling nearly half off an upper bunk, poised for a neck-cracking fall. Ranging, slovenly, and congenitally heedless, David was the child who could break their hearts, who, predictably, might perish in a crumpled wreck or a misapplied fraternity stunt. "The kid needs to close a few hatches," he said. "Sometimes I can't believe he and Sarah are related."

Though David might careen and stumble through life, their first-born, they could be sure, would walk a narrow path. She had always been the careful one, always colored within the lines; in her quiet way she would always keep herself in balance, coast in smooth rotations through the procession of the years.

"The only problem with Sarah is that she needs to come out of her shell a bit."

In her reserve and timidity, their daughter seemed the product of dilute jism, a meager quotient of spunk. It pained them both that she could not be more animated, more engaging. "We should get her to join an improv group," Adam suggested, "or Toastmasters."

"*That* will be the day!" As if propelled upwards by the impetus, the hard-packed judgmentalism of this scoff, Marion rose and resumed her tour of the room. Turning, she surveyed the collection of chinoiserie that occupied the mantel. "Sarah hates to perform," she continued, in a more modulated voice. "Remember, in sixth grade, how she played one of the Lost Boys? They gave her two lines to say, and she was petrified for weeks."

Adam uncrossed his legs and leaned forward in his seat. He entertained the notion to imitate, to stand also; his wife's restlessness had lapped over onto him. "I just hope she finds someone who treats her well," he said resignedly.

Marion grasped a tureen, lowered it towards herself, read "Spode" off the base. Piece-by-piece, she was acquiring confidence in the Bents' tastes. "She's choosey," she said, putting it back. "I'm sure she'll pick the right one."

"It's what happens after that that concerns me. Can she keep him interested? Marriage is a long haul."

Marion heard her womanhood, the nectarous female principle which passes from mother to daughter, being challenged. Protectively, she felt the instinct to jut her physical presence, her treasury of persuasive curves and hollows, into the discussion. Turning and swooping, she alighted on the vacant ottoman opposite Adam's chair. Drawing herself erect, her breasts welling against her plain cotton top, she asserted: "She'll do fine."

"How can you be so sure?"

She peered beyond him, toward the horizon: an oracular pose. "A mother knows."

"I beg to differ. There are some things about Sarah not even you can know."

"Such as?"

Adam observed a level, competent set to his wife's features. She had pulled her hair back this morning and looked prim and businesslike, every bit the schoolmarm. He had imagined they would have this conversation—if at all—in the dark; to be broaching it by daylight struck him as remotely unseemly. "How good she is in bed, for instance."

"Adam!"

"Hear me out." Pausing, he tented his fingers, signaling the launch of a Socratic argument. "Don't you think we owe it to her to talk about the nitty-gritty?"

"You think our daughter's a prude?"

"How do I know? How do you? My guess is that she's a steady B, just as in everything else. What I do know is that people can get bored with each other sexually. I don't want her to lose the fish out of the net."

"So—you want to teach her about technique?"

In dispensing fatherly advice, he had always thought of himself as having been frank, timely, and thorough. With Sarah he had had ample opportunity—on slow-moving chairlifts, when alone with her in the car—to rail against tattoos and tailgating, intemperance and early pregnancy. But he had never thought it his place to explicate the contents of the *Kama Sutra.* "No," he said, "but I was hoping you would."

Marion suppressed a snort: she had been perfectly baited, drawn to the hook. "Well," she reflected, "I don't remember my mother ever assessing *my* skills."

"There was no need; you were a natural."

Another point for him. This conversation had the aspect of a chess game: he had surprised her with his rook. "Flatterer."

"No, just being honest. You've always been good in the clinches."

She did not doubt his sincerity. Undraped, her body had never failed to entice him, and obligingly, she had placed few restrictions on its use. "Sex is easy," she declared breezily. "It surprises me that so many women find it a chore."

"Those are the Puritans, honey. There are plenty of them still out there. I see them at the office: They don't have orgasms; they have fibromyalgia."

"Pity on them. They lose out both ways."

At this close proximity and theatrically positioned, they sensed something building up between them: static, a field. Sexuality, their bodies insisted, remained a given, an unalterable premise; neither of them had aged to such a state of hormonal depletion that they could ignore its petitions. Yet they also knew that what they would have to retrieve, if they were to stay together, was simple lightheartedness, the quality of being at ease with each other. No more coercive

77

encounters; no more punitive refusals. Sex should be a lark, pure and unaffected fun.

Adam reached forward and squeezed her nearer trapezius, simulating an exam. "Any tenderness?"

"None."

"See?" he quipped, "you're just the opposite. Everything about you works just fine."

And now, helplessly—acquiescently—she smiled. He was, undeniably, the only man who had ever owned her. Others had been granted easements, but only he had secured the rights to pluck and till. After so many years any new lover would seem a trespasser, a brigand. Abruptly, she was glad he still held title. Grasping his hand, she praised, "Having a stud for a husband has been good for my health."

A white lie, he knew. Countless furtive comparisons, sidelong glances down locker room aisles and over urinal rims had brought home the truth: He was smaller than most. Occasionally he had been able to persuade himself that the other men she had been with—he had never asked for an exact count—had been similarly deficient, or that her recall of their dimensions had, mercifully, faded over time; more often he sought solace in the possibility that, as the joke went, It wasn't the club, it was the stroke. "I tried to please," he sighed.

"You have," she promised, "you have." He had made his case well, she realized: you couldn't overlook the basics; a couple must know how to pleasure each other. "I'll talk to Sarah," she said.

"What have you whipped up for us this morning, Clarence?"

"Oh, pretty standard fare. Porridge for the doctor, eggs for the missus. And bread, of course."

"Of course."

"Try a piece first…Sometimes it goes better before everything else."

There: a nervous expectancy, concern. Something. They both heard it; they had heard it yesterday and the day before. Whenever Clarence spoke of the humble, unadorned loaf which seemed an obligate component of each morning's repast, there was a tonal shift, a wash of preoccupation in his voice.

Adam managed a faint, polite smile. "I've always believed in following the chef's recommendations," he said, summoning forbearance. Should he ask for jam or butter? he wondered while waiting to be served. Though this would have been the obvious expedient, he felt oddly restrained from doing so, as if deterred by a subliminal taboo. Thus, when the bread was offered and he brought it to his mouth, he was, once again, set to feign approval, but quite unprepared to encounter this: a lighter, airier texture; a complexly wholesome, multi-grain taste; and even a hint of moist warmth, the comforting heatedness of a loaf just baked.

By mid-morning the sky had turned a clarion shade of blue; beckoned by the crisp, clear air, they agreed to a stroll. Following the spine of the island they passed through pungent stands of cedar and pine, then came to a swale set between two rocky knolls. From the launch on Sunday Marion had imagined that the land at this point formed a saddle shaped to the buttocks of Titans. "Look!" she exclaimed, pointing down from the crest.

"What is it?"

"A garden."

Adam peered into the glen, expecting to find ordered rows, discrete beds. "Not much of one," he judged.

"It's a nature-garden, silly; nothing else makes any sense out here. Don't you see how they've planted the banks with shrubs?"

Adam had never been adept at hidden image problems; radiology was not his long suit. Slowly he discerned patches of euonymus and lilac, bands of juniper and forsythia. "You're right," he granted. "Let's have a closer look."

They descended an overgrown path to the bottom of the hollow, discovering there, in a small cleared area, a pair of Adirondack chairs set on either side of a flat-topped rock.

"What a lovely little nook!" Marion proclaimed, easing into one of the seats.

Adam sat down in the other. "It's the perfect sanctuary," he agreed, panning the scene. This was, he gauged the creation of a landscape architect, a clever farrago of wild and cultivated plants. "I wish we had this at home."

Their property in Quidnunquit was a three-quarter-acre parcel, clustered with others of a similar size onto an obsessively maintained comma punctuating the southern sweep of Massachusetts Bay. The watery vistas they and their neighbors enjoyed came at no small price of privacy; privet hedges and white-stained fences notwithstanding, every house on the Point offered a voyeuristic view, from its upper floor, of all that transpired out-of-doors on the adjacent lots. Whenever they had cocktails on the deck or laid themselves out to sun or played lawn games, their leisure was marred by the awareness that the Rineharts on the right or the Cunninghams on the left could be looking on: leering, envying, disapproving.

"She comes here often; I can feel her presence."

"Who?"

"The matriarch. Mrs. Bent."

Over the years, he had learned to let her claim such intimations without contesting them. Perhaps his faith in hard logic, the scientific method, had loosened; or perhaps, in his maturity, he had come to accept that all our lives front on the ineffable, the mysterious. And, as to what lay beyond this frontier, he was glad to have her as his scout. In the manner of a blind man questioning the sighted, he asked, "What does she do here?"

"Oh, she reads, she recoups. Her husband joins her sometimes, but she prefers to be alone. This is her place apart."

"I feel like we're intruding."

Beside him, he heard her inhale deeply and hold it; it was as if she was filtering the vale's still, textured air, its embroidery of scents, for

ЁЁ

guidance—a directive. "No, I don't think so. She's a generous woman; she wouldn't begrudge others the peace she finds here."

Above them, beyond a canopy of lazily swaying branches, the sun seemed to meander through the sky. Lifting his face to it, he searched for the angle that would yield a measure of warmth. "I'm happy to hear that," he said, letting his weight sink fully into the chair. "Peace is a hard thing to come by."

For a moment they let nature spill over them—the hum of the insects, the patter of the birds, the susurrations of the breeze—and in this brief, unheralded interval they seemed to make a transition into the next iteration, a new phase.

At length it was Marion who spoke, offering an apology. "I've been unfair to you all these years," she said. Her tone was declarative, actively contrite.

"How?"

"I expected you to make up for my dad."

One of the darker motifs of Marion's emotional life was that she had never found a way to ground herself with her father, never touched the bedrock of unconditional love. Though set in more acidic soil, her rootedness with her mother was firmer, more secure. "I tried for a while," he recalled, "after I realized what was missing between the two of you."

"A penis, you mean. He never got over the fact that I didn't have one."

Adam had long ago reached the conclusion that her father had been a clinical type, one of those blustering, inwardly desperate men who, having amounted to something in boyhood, choose to linger there too long. In Mathew Scott's case, the hook, the corrupting influence, had been hockey. A first-line left-winger at Bowdoin, he had spent the half-dozen year after graduation trying to deke his way into the NHL. When he finally gave up the chase, Julia Phillips—the rich girl with a father who dangled a sinecure in front of him—had been there to catch him. "Your dad had a dynastic complex," he consoled. "Having a daughter wasn't part of the plan."

Marion's thoughts slipped back to a node in time, a memory still laden with hurt. On a shimmering Chicago summer afternoon, a day when the air hung heavy with the down of milkweed and the agitation of cicadas, she had prepared lemonade. Her father would be thirsty when he came home, she had conceived; he would enjoy sitting on the terrace and drinking something cool. She had prepared everything herself: the pitcher, the ice bucket, the plate of vanilla wafers; she had placed the provisions on a glass-topped table set (like this rock) between two chairs—one for her, one for him—then watched over it, deflecting flies, attentively waiting. But when he had appeared he was not, as she had imagined, dressed in pinstripes and wingtips; instead he had burst forth, baseball glove in hand, part of a three-ringed commotion, leading her brothers out onto the lawn. After a short, raucous game, George and Harry had slurped up most of the lemonade. And her father's sole gesture of thanks, if it had really been that, had been to tousle her forelocks with his sweaty palm. Even now she could feel this dampness, the residue of his indifference, smeared across her brow. "Weak men feel propped up by having sons," she conceded.

"Exactly. I'd like two or three more myself."

"Stop it, Adam. I forgive my father for who he was and wasn't; I forgive you."

Her words were not sourced as usual. In their ordinary badinage she seemed to retrieve each remark from a cache at the front of her mind and sling it at him; for years her consciousness had been quiver-full of quips and cuts. This "I forgive you," however, had risen up through the meat of her, from a source more proximate to her soul.

"You do?"

She turned and looked at him obliquely and thought of the other men, the lead players, who had vied to be here, midway through life, coupled with her: Paul, the pudgy Jew from Scarsdale, her first love, now a patent attorney; Chip, the crew captain from Penn with the Herculean physique but scarcely a neuron to spare; and Victor, the artiste, who probably would have won her had he known not to hit. The way we select a mate, she mused, resembled her own sparing method of beachcombing: regardless of how many finds you turn up, by rule, in the end, you can bring home only one. "I do," she echoed.

In his waking dreams, Adam sometimes liked to imagine that they were not real, incarnate beings but protagonists in an unfinished work of fiction—originally a romance, now a tragi-comedy—and that their every conversation, every exchange, advanced the story by a paragraph, or a section. The denouement, he had long assumed, would be bittersweet, a parting assuaged by its final, weary uncontestedness, and by compensatory Nietzschean overtones, a coda endorsing the theme of personal transcendence. But now, as his wife spoke, he saw editor's marks upon the text, whole chapters nixed. "I didn't expect this," he admitted.

Internally, Marion detected an ebbing tide, an exodus of bile. "I'm not angry anymore," she perceived.

"About—"

"About everything. About nothing. *You* know; you've had to live with it all these years. I stored up all this venom. I thought I needed it for protection. Now I see that I don't, that I never did."

"Keep going," he prompted. "Convince me that I'm really hearing this." He surveyed his wife's face, her habitus, for some noticeable change; the physician in him needed corroboration, signs trending with symptoms. But what was the physiognomy of a broken spirit? His years in the consulting room had not taught him this, nor how to confirm the presence of healing.

"It's hard to describe," she said. "I guess I don't feel deprived anymore. I've lost my agenda. I'm at ease."

Relaxedness: We lose the aptitude for it as we go along, he thought. We're too busy chasing after loftier titles, fatter paychecks, fancier domiciles—all the brummagem components of the American Dream—to slow down, kick back, simply be. Like most of her girlfriends, Marion had tried all the standard nostrums—aromatherapy, herbal baths, an occasional Xanax—not finding anything that would stick. Just an hour or two of mellowness, a little buzz, was all she seemed to get from them, and then she was back to being herself: nervous and overwrought. But what struck him about her present mood was that it had not been procured; she had not consumed anything to induce it. "This *is* progress," he confirmed. "You're overcoming conflict."

"It's taken long enough, hasn't it?"

With his eyes closed to the sun, he let his head loll in her direction. "And for that," he said softly, "I forgive *you.*"

Hi, this is Susan. I can't answer the phone right now; hopefully that's because I'm out doing something serious people would disapprove of. If you leave me a message after the—

"Dead again," she muttered. In the earpiece she heard only scratching noises, electronic dross. By now, she had sampled all of the island's highest points with the same result: Each time, the connection had failed. Evidently there were still places left where cell phones just didn't work.

So: while she was here there would be no chit-chat, no reporting in to her girlfriends. For a week, she supposed she could endure it.

How long, his sin of omission? Two months? Three? Unconscionable. The mole over her left triceps seemed to be broadening. Ever since he had known her it had had the appearance of a miniature molasses cookie; slightly raised, the width of a pencil eraser, he knew it well, this dollop of melanin. In those days when her flesh was a fervent vastness which his lips freely explored, he had thought of it a waypoint, a wee sepia isle where he could obtain his bearings, linger. But recently he had been noticing signs of tectonic disruption. Its center, once smooth, had developed a crack, a scarcely visible fault line dividing it into two approximate halves. Its shape, also, had changed: on one side it had acquired a curling pointedness; among the familiar islands it had come to resemble Barbados or Saint Kitts.

He had failed to alert her to these observations—why? Had he simply been too preoccupied, too caught up in his own angst to caution her? Or was the real explanation more sinister? By and large, he left dermatology to dermatologists, but as much as any physician he heeded the ABCD's: appearance, border, color, diameter. A change in one was suspicious; in two it was presumptive. Before now he should have had Marion see Jim Feldman, alias Dr. Sunspot; instead he had dared a melanoma to sprout. Narcissistic injury—what the shrinks called it—could be a dangerous thing. Murder-suicide occasionally the outcome. More often, something like this: a brake check omitted, a prescription allowed to lapse. Dark deeds, all.

The consolation in this self-examination, he realized, was the very fact that he was making it. Whatever suppressed rage it was that had dulled the reflexes of his conscience must be diminishing. He was recouping, thankfully, his proper self. Further, judging by the myriad similar lesions that had passed through his practice, the consequences of his inaction would be few. Marion's growth was at an early stage; if it was precancerous it could be excised. She would be fine. He would see to it.

On the brink of the precipice Adam inhaled deeply, crouched, lunged. Arms forward and eyes wide open, he hurtled towards his target, the largest swell in the series, with the willfulness of a last-chance tackler. *No rocks please,* he prayed, in the instant before touching. *Let it go on.* Then he sliced into the cool jade ocean, down a dozen feet or more, to a depth where the sunlight became a mere golden smear across a green translucency. Exhaling, he leveled off, and staying under, squid-stroked his way back towards shore. *Might see a striper or tautog in here.* Finally, lungs burning, he popped to the surface, her churlish seal.

"Bravo!"

Above, Marion sat perched in a cleft in the granite; from his perspective, she was mostly haunches. To be viewed from such an angle would have been anathema to many of the other Quidnunquit wives, their rumps grown doughy and dimpled with the years, but his remained girlishly unabashed, comfortable with all takes. "How was my form?" he called, bobbing in a trough. As an adolescent she taken diving lessons, and from this training, she retained a repertoire of gainers and twists which were still obligingly performed, at the request of friends, in selected venues.

"Everything was good except the head position. You have to stop looking at the water."

Not possible: to knife through space and not look up—down, actually. Yet, in this sport, to peek was to flinch. Wittingly, he lied: "I keep forgetting to do that."

"Try it again!" she exhorted. Adam was far enough below her that his untanned body appeared specimen-like, a bug in broth. "Do you need a hand?"

"I can make it, thanks."

She looked on, arms-around-knees, as he neared the bluff, selected handholds, and heaved himself onto a ledge. In the interval while he lay there, prone and resting, she considered him, detachedly, as a quantity of flesh, fresh catch on the dock; no doubt he would have been tasty basted in lemon sauce, as savory as swordfish. When he stood his chest was mottled, tenderized by pressure marks. "Be careful coming up," she warned.

"I know, slippery when wet."

Adam made a cautious, four-point ascent to where she was sitting, holding his body close to the contour. As she observed his physique working, muscles and sinews passing in an out of relief, she felt a flush, a faint libidinal tide, running beneath her skin; it was as if she were reliving that breathless yet since-forgotten inflection point in adolescence when, while watching the athletic exertions of some half-stripped classmate, she had first become conscious of desire. "Towel?" she asked, when he had completed the climb.

"Thanks." Before taking it, he wriggled and shook himself in the fashion of a freestyler readying himself for the start. For many men his age, especially the paunchy, cigar-chomping lot she saw strolling the golf course every weekend, these actions would have been unflattering, an unsightly flapping of the flab. But with a desultory exercise regimen—tennis if he could scare up a singles game; bike rides to Hull or Scituate if he could not; squash and pond hockey during the winter—Adam had kept the growth in his girth to two or three belt notches; he was still passably sleek.

"Are you refreshed?"

Finding level ground, he turned and scanned a section of main as if seeking a prompt, a rubric inscribed below the horizon. They were at the southwest corner of the island; it was mid-afternoon. "Better than that," he observed. "I feel intact."

Head back, Marion faced with him into the wind and took a deep breath, inhaling richness. "That's what happens to a person up here, isn't it?"

"You feel it"—pausing, he canted his head and, with a flattened palm, tried to knock the brine out of an ear canal—"too?"

As a casual student of the arts, Marion had always favored sharp-edged constructions. Complex tones, ambiguous themes, subtle shadings: she had never understood the appeal of these methods. Her emotional life itself, however, had become a blurry canvas, the likeness of a DeKooning; yet at the core of it she was beginning to detect an emerging coherence. "I do," she said.

He smoothed his hair back, considering. "It must be the climate. All those wives' tales about the benefits of the sea air."

"I wonder if there's been any research on the subject, maybe in the public health literature."

During his training she had perused enough medical journals, coffee-stained copies of *The Lancet* and *JAMA* to acquire a working knowledge of statistics. In those days they had sometimes filled the hours, the lazy intervals between sex and more sex, with earnest talk of chi square values and confidence intervals. These discussions had unearthed, beneath the nappy, society-girl façade, an intellect as nimble as his; from them he had derived a vain assurance that his genes would be well-paired. "Getting a grant would be hard," he predicted. Lifting his arms, he formed a bracket, and read within it: "Proposed: In this study we will endeavor to ascertain…how many weeks on a Maine island…are necessary and sufficient…to normalize the bowel habits…of a cohort of personal injury lawyers."

CHARLES DENBY

"Impossible man!" Furling the towel still in her lap, she snapped it at him, almost connecting.

"'Feeling my oats!" he crowed, withholding a riposte. "Yes, I'm feeling well indeed. Never better! We should have booked another week."

Using her palm as a visor, she studied him, *homo sapiens,* refulgent and statuesque beneath the three o'clock sun. His symmetrical, wide-footed pose called to mind one of those transparent, standing models packed with removable viscera from which, as children, we are encouraged to learn anatomy. It would be expedient, she thought, to disassemble him, examine his inner organs for wear. If only men came with warranties! Long years of widowhood she feared. "Maybe next year," she said.

They both heard it, this cautious, sidling move towards recommitment, and having heard it, let it marinate within a gap, a brief frightened stoppage in the conversation.

"This isn't anything like what I imagined," she resumed, panning her gaze across the blue ebullience of the outer Bay. "I thought I would be stuck on some crowded little slab at the end of a causeway. Everything's gotten so overbuilt. The Vineyard is wall-to-wall people. Nantucket's almost as bad. I didn't think there were any private places left."

"This is one of them."

As though summoned to action by this affirmation, Marion rose and unclasped her barrette. Set loose, her hair revealed more of the auburn tints, the Celtic accents that it took on in summer. "Are you going in again?" she asked.

Observing his wife in profile through the clear air, Adam felt suddenly proud. Was there anything better to hold the eye, he wondered, that this fine, willful, intelligent, well-bred woman? "You bet," he replied. "One more plunge."

"In that case, I'd better show you how it's done."

Then, abruptly, she tossed off her smock, soft-footed down to the launch point, looked, and leapt. Through a perfect arc his eye followed her down until she struck the water, head straight, toes together, and slipped beneath the waves…

Within a field of monograms a single given name—LAURA—
obtruded. Crude block letters, sans-serif, interpolated among faithfully
rendered fonts. Some impetuous adolescent immortalizing his first
conquest. A family tradition flouted. Desecration or not, the galaxy of
letters carved into the picnic table top awoke in Adam warming
memories of his campfire days: all those formative hours spent
marking up wood—a city boy crafting his manhood, notch-by-notch.

To the job at hand. He spread a dishtowel across the weathered
two-by-fours and, over this, inverted his dop kit. A homey chore away
from home. Who says men don't take care of their things? True, he
tended to perform tasks this humdrum—trimming nasal hair, removing
lint, sewing up rents—only when no other diversion presented itself;
otherwise, to a fault, he awaited Marion's prods, her piqued notices
that he had violated some arguable rule of hygiene or orderliness. He
was not, after all, a fop.

There was more detritus admixed with his toiletries than he had
anticipated: pill fragments, half-dissolved lozenges, granola kernels,
and a light, harlequin sediment. Entropy's grist. Raking and sifting, he
separated this refuse out and brushed it aside; what remained required
sorting. His kit, more compartmentalized than most, featured snug
pockets and sleeves, a retentive inner architecture. First, he cleaned
the larger items—electric shaver, comb, toothbrush, tube of Crest—
and returned them to their proper place. This left a scree of curiosities,
a scratchy, jangling mass of artifacts, haphazardly kept, passively
retained. For ease of identification he spread them out; the heap
became a collage. *What archeologists must do,* he thought. *Slow,
tedious work. Lucky for them the Sumerians didn't have all this
stuff. Match books, little bars of soap, shampoo and
conditioner—no hotels to purloin them from. They did have coins,
though—ah, what's this?*

Amidst a clutch of pennies he found a two-toned interloper, bronze
in the center, silver at the rim. "RF," he read, and then, in the minuscule

superscript, *"Liberte, Egalite, Fraternite."* A token, admitting him to a memory. Paris—had it been eight years ago? After they had introduced the Euro, as this one proved. He recalled the scent of lilacs drying after a rain, the cry and hubbub of the farmers' markets. How they had sauntered along the ancient alleys, down the cobblestone lanes, feeling ripe, never better. Bent together, no less a pair than any other, from Montmartre to Montparnasse, from the Marais to the Musée D'Orsay, they had traced, during those five days, the parameters of the still-possible, an outline of sustainable romance. Acutely, he lamented that they had not been back since: either to Paris, or to that polis, that nexus, that meeting ground of the affections, where one feels whole.

All couples have their cycles, he mused, rolling the coin between his fingers. Each begins with the hope that we can start over again, that we can be as we were. We blot out the bad times; we tuck away the resentments; we squelch the sarcasm. We put on our best Ozzie-and-Harriet faces. Then we resume the soft talk and the nuzzling, the dinners out and the mornings in. Our children, who have doubted our prospects, are reassured. Our better friends notice, also. They wonder if we have been to a clinic or a spa. And if it is something that we are taking, they want to take it, too.

Marion, he vowed, *if we can put ourselves back together, I'll make it stick. I'll warrant that. I won't let us trip up again. I'll festoon you with gems and shower you with trifles. The love notes won't stop. We'll take moonlight walks and escape to urban trysts. We'll learn Italian together. We'll skinny-dip indiscreetly. Whatever comes, I'll treat you sweetly. Such is my pledge to the girl that I adore. As a bride you've bloomed for me many times. All I ask is that you do so once more.*

Back inside, at the head of the bed, he found a note. Instantly his heart raced; he felt trepidation, a rush of terror. She was calling it off, he knew; this flirtation with hope, their effort at repair. It was simply too late for them—how could he have thought otherwise? You can only neglect what is frail and animate so long before it fails. Unnerved, he opened the paper and read:

> *Darling—*
>
> *I observed you tidying up your affairs, so to speak, and didn't want to disturb you. I'm off chasing after crustaceans, lounging with limpets. Back by six. Looking forward to twilight cocktails.*
>
> > *Tender kisses,*
> > *M.*

Ooops! Didn't see that one coming. Rogue wavelet. Now I'll have a wet bottom. Damp undies, too. The water's so clear in these pools. Must be why the fish avoid them. Not so much as a mummichaug in here. Plenty of clams, though. And periwinkles, too. Everything's gray, green, or black, except the sea stars. Little tidal super supernovae. The northern ocean's so dark. Must say I prefer the Caribbean: all those angelfish, tangs, and wrasses. More entertaining than mollusks. The way they glide along, watching, waiting. Not unlike men, really. Men always hankering after the basics. A meal. A profit. A pussy. But, being honest, where's the blame in that? A man is a man, a fish is a fish. Enjoy them for what they are. God's creations. Funny to think of Adam that way. He has the right name for it, though. Wouldn't he look adorable in a fig leaf? Fat chance. He won't even wear a Speedo. Doesn't think he stacks up. I've tried to tell him he's fine. With a woman you just have to press the right buttons. And he does. Puts pressure up toward the top of me. Hits the exact spot. And his body's fit to the task. Slim in the hips and broad up above. Strong jaw, too. Very strong. Like a parrotfish. Nothing better than how he kissed me in the beginning. How he still does, if I let him. Ooo! There's a thought that makes me shiver. Do you see that, my parrotfish? After all this time you can still raise my quills: you still give me gooseflesh...

"Clarence, can I pick your brain?"

"Better that than pickle it."

"I'm looking for a reading recommendation."

"By all means: read as much as possible."

The old man's humor, Marion was learning, was as dry, as spare, as his physique. More than that, she was beginning to suspect that there was something elastic about his intellect, as if he could adapt himself to the discussion of any subject, at any level. "I do, I do," she said, "but I'd like your advice on what's good—there's so much out there."

Clarence was at the counter, preparing hors-d'oeuvres; Marion had stopped in to add ice to her drink.

"Well, I SEE"—antic stress, extra nasality, applied to this word— "that you're reading Jane Austen. Do you like the pre-Victorians?"

"Oh, mostly as an alternative to medication, if I'm in a state. Otherwise I prefer prose that's a little more stimulating."

"That's how we gauge a book isn't it? by what effect it produces."

Nibbling on a cucumber slice, Marion deliberated. The conversation, she saw, was taking a rhetorical turn. "Yes, I suppose you could say that."

"And how long does it stay with you, this effect, after you've read it?"

"Not long, usually, since I'm always moving on to the next one. I probably read a book a week."

The chef's tone darkened. "If books were nourishment you'd be subsisting on candy."

"I don't follow you."

Without interrupting his work the chef propounded this distinction: "There are two types of books, I would submit. There are books that entertain—murder mysteries, spy thrillers, horror novels—and there are books that illuminate. By that I mean they instruct or elevate in some way. All are stories, but only the latter can be called literature. Only literature produces a lingering effect; only literature sustains us."

Culpably, Marion sighed. "I must be reading only stories, then. Nothing really seems to stick with me."

"That's the condition of modern fiction, Mrs. Falk. Books used to be savored; now they're just consumed."

"Like everything else in the culture."

"People don't buy hardcover anymore."

"But surely there're one or two you can recommend: books that aren't pap."

Clarence looked up from his cutting board; wide-eyed, he appeared to behold something far away. "Among the works of the known greats, I would read *Love in the Time of Cholera*, first and foremost, and as for the up-and-comers, Amos Burroway has great promise."

Marion puzzled. "I don't think I've heard of him."

"You wouldn't have, just yet. Stay tuned."

"I can't believe how late it stays light up here."

"I know. It seems like we had dinner hours ago."

Through the lavender dusk Adam cast his gaze east, and thought of Ireland.

They would be sleeping now: the pub keepers, the shop stewards, the farmers, and all the other citizens of Ballyferriter, that pleasing hamlet. How many faces, he wondered, would they recognize after all these years? Certainly Mrs. Nolan—Lydia, was it?—the kindly B & B owner who had taken them in, two skinny kids roaming the Gaelic counties on bicycles; also the loquacious, pipe-smoking gillie they had hired, on a whim, for half a day, and perhaps two or three more, ruddy-countenanced all. As much as the grandparents one knows only briefly as a child, he longed to see them again, that puckish lot, for they had shared a time of innocence, of insouciance; they had peopled the landscape of better days. "Do you know what I like most about this place?" he asked, swirling the last of his nightcap.

Marion sat next to him, one leg drawn up to her chest, examining the plume of her cigarette as it ascended into the eaves. For soporific effect, in recent months, she had added an after-dinner smoke. "What?"

"The longitude. We're so far away from most of America; Europe seems so close."

She knew this mood, this theme. Adam's other life—the one he had not lived—had been spent as an artist, or a correspondent, or, most unrepentantly, as a vagabond on the other side of the Atlantic. His handful of trips abroad—the obligatory schoolboy tour, their honeymoon, and a pair of sojourns to Greece and France—had provided the thread, out of which he had woven whole cloth, the adventures of an expatriate alter ego, a footloose bachelor who ranged from Glasgow to Naples, from Madrid to Kiev, in pursuit of the bright, sumptuous edge of culture, *la dolce vita*. Within this persona he was capable of affectionately yearning for vistas he had never seen, piazzas and monuments known to him only from the travel section. "They're having a hot summer in the UK," she told him. "The Highlanders are wilting in their tartans."

"I was just thinking of our time in Ireland. It wasn't like that when we were there."

She took a fresh puff, savored it, let it go. "Hardly. It rained a lot."

"Just about every afternoon, and we were thankful for it; the showers kept us cool."

"All that moisture brought out the slugs. Do you remember?"

They were entering, together, what only a few days before would have been prohibited terrain. No couple, in sundering, speaks of the good times.

"Of course. It was just about this time of evening. We tried cutting across a field."

"When I saw them I screamed bloody murder—"

"And jumped on my back." Vividly, he recalled a noisy pantomime of lovemaking: her arms and legs clamping his torso, her whimpering cries, her hands scrabbling at his chest. "You were hysterical," he said.

"I couldn't help it. They were such *hide*ous creatures!"

"They looked like big, uncircumcised phalluses."

With her free hand she delivered a censoring jab to his ribs.

"It's true!" he persisted. "I'm not trying to be Freudian. I had to watch where I was stepping; I got a much better look at them."

In acknowledgment or apology, she nestled up to him, setting her head gently into the hollow of his shoulder. "My rescuer," she purred. "You carried me all the way back to the inn; it must have been a mile or more."

"And afterwards," he continued, raising his glass in front of them, "we had to knock back a few of these to get you calmed down."

Steadfastness, a quiet reliability under pressure: It was a part of Adam that few people knew. Unadvertised, behind the country-club manner and the August bloodline, there was dense structure, real spine. Once, on a trip to the Berkshires, they had been first-to-the-scene at a one-car accident, a subcompact, nose-down in a culvert; inside, two boys, half-conscious and indeterminately injured, lay slumped against the dash, pinned there by a welter of objects displaced in the crash. Unhesitatingly, as smoke billowed from under the hood, he had effected a frantic rescue, clearing away the refuse and evacuating the boys. Not three minutes later, before the arrival of any rescue personnel, the car had ignited into a burning pyre. "You've always taken good care of me, Adam," she said.

"I've tried."

"You did everything right up to a certain point."

"Which was?"

"When you allowed me to think I might have it better elsewhere; when you let me doubt."

Pensively, he sifted the gathering starlight for an explanation. "I've always been lousy at self-promotion," he conceded. "Mea culpa."

"I guess I thought that if you didn't believe in us, then I didn't believe in us—that's where I started to let go."

Reaching up, he curved his fingers around the nape of her neck, splaying them into her soft mane. "I almost let you slip away, didn't I?"

And again they came, unchecked this time, the sweet hot tears of release, of catharsis. She let them run down her cheeks in parallel rivulets; she let them fall undeflected onto her shoulder, his. "Will you catch me now, Adam?" she blurted.

"I will," he promised in a whisper. "I will."

THURSDAY

Omit nothing. That was the analyst's mantra, wasn't it? *Say what's on your mind as it is in your mind; omit nothing.* He understood how it might avail at a time like this. Working through conflict, vetting ambivalence. For, if he did stay, he should do so out of a unity of intention; if he remained, he should do so whole-heartedly.

An exercise, then. Gathering himself, he closed his eyes, and under his breath, said this: "Not so fast! You're only forty-two. Young enough to have a second wife—a second life. You have options to consider. Assuming the marriage can be saved, should it? Devilish question. Necessary polemic. For a minute, take the opposing view. Sometimes a reshuffling's the right thing to do. Friends of yours, cases in point. Sam, for sure. Best thing he ever did was leave his first bride. Fat little bore, she was. Now he's got Ellen. His titty Texas trophy. Bet she keeps him up nights. And Harry. Whole rotating harem around him. What a whoremaster! Milking the college grads' singles' clubs like a pro. New one on his arm every time we see him. Doubtful he'll tie the knot again. Having too much fun philandering, and why not? Served out his time until the last kid was in college, then off with the ball and chain. He had the right...You do, too, Falk. Fly the coop if you like. No telling where it might lead. Plenty of lonely hens around looking for a drake. Laura Schwartz has made her interest clear. Bedding a J.A.P. would be different. Probably talks the whole time. Drops her nail file at the end. Or, for a challenge of sorts, you could road test Roberta. Rubenesque and then some. Himalayan breasts. A pity the ass is proportionate...Living alone has its plusses, too. Do what you want. Watch TV in bed. Eat soup out of the can. Belch. Fart. Regress. Be a man..."

No, he thought, curtailing his soliloquy, *that's not what you're thinking. What you're thinking is*—like a person enduring a spike of pain, he rolled onto his side in the bed, clutching a pillow—*is Marion, Marion. You, my dearest. Still you.*

June 24ᵗʰ
Hi Judy!

You must think I'm bored, writing to you a second time, but that's far from the truth. Actually, my time up here has gotten more and more intriguing—I wish you were here to give advice.

Do you remember how it was when you were first with Frank? There's that slightly-out-of-breath feeling that you carry around. And a funny electrical sensation that seems to run through all you nerves. Well, that's the state I've been in the past couple of days. It's not a fever, and I'm on the near side of menopause. There's more: When I look at Adam he seems unfamiliar, like a man I'm just getting involved with. I notice his fine bone structure and (your favorite) those long eyelashes as if I'm just discovering his body, exploring all the parts. The truth is I feel excited, confused, timid, afraid. My emotions are a whirlpool, and you're not here to help me straighten them out. I really don't know if I'm coming or going.

I haven't shared any of this with Adam, of course. That's a woman's prerogative, isn't it? Don't tip your hand in the beginning. Make sure the guy has fallen for you. I'm assuming he'll come back to me. He's a doctor, after all. They're patient by nature; they want to see things mend.

The risk is that I've hurt him too much, pushed him away for too long.

It worries me, strangely, that we have only three days left. Even though I'm married to him, I have this crazy sense of running out of time. I feel like I've met a man on vacation and we'll be getting on different planes Sunday. If there's magic in the air we have to grasp it now.

At the movies this is the part where my mouth gets dry. How will it turn out? Will they fall for each other (again)? I'm on the edge of my seat.

Pass the popcorn, sister.

> *Anxiously,*
> *Marion*

"Ah, my Endymion!"

"Yes, I've risen from my cave." At the threshold of the living room Adam paused, attempting to massage his eyes into full focus. "What time is it?" he asked.

"Almost nine. I was about to go in and shake you."

"It must be the change in the weather. It's gotten soupy, hasn't it?"

Overnight, it had turned warm and humid and still; the doldrums, fingering northerly, had reached them. Ordinarily they each adapted poorly to such conditions. Adam became sluggish and dull-witted, an adagio distortion of himself; Marion grew restless, bored, insomniac. But this morning they both felt fresh and even-tempered; their susceptibility to the lower barometric range seemed diminished. "I've been up for a while," she told him.

"What have you been doing?"

"Oh, girl stuff. I wrote a letter; now I'm going through some of the catalogues I brought along."

One of her most intractable quirks was a disdain, nearly a phobia, for the traditional shopping experience. The clamor and jostle of the malls, their clashing tides of impetuous adolescents, dawdling welfare recipients, and harried soccer moms was anathema to her; the department store culture—its hollow image-creation and obsequious salesmanship—afforded no relief; even the local shops, where she was cosseted by the blue-hairs, the South Coast's dithering dowagers, failed to satisfy her need for remove, a private space where she could sample new plumage. Had she lived in the days before mail order, he believed, she would have managed like a woman down on her luck, making her wardrobe, once complete, last a lifetime. *"That's* why your suitcase was so heavy," he ribbed, marveling amusedly at her planful streak. "Have you found anything you like?"

At a pace expressing exasperation she flipped a page, then another. "I'm not sure yet. I could use a few new tops."

Dawning to an opportunity, a chance to better his spousal deportment, he entered the room and made his way behind the chair where she was sitting; when he displayed interest, feigned or not, in this sort of mundanity, she gave him credit for the effort.

"I like what you have on," he ventured. "You should clone it in aqua or cornflower blue." She was wearing a sleeveless, off-white cotton blouse; her upper arms, lightly freckled, were evenly tanned. What was it about the cut, the design, of this species of garment, he wondered, that had always affected him so? Did it render her more desirable, this extra hand-span of revealed flesh? Or did it spawn an association to his mother, all those summer days he had watched her toiling bare-armed amid the marigolds and the nasturtiums? Perhaps one like it had even clinched the argument that she was the one to marry, a sufficient approximation of the archetype. "It gives you a classic look," he said.

"You have old-fashioned tastes, my darling."

"Admittedly." And then, reverently, from shoulder to elbow and back up again, he stroked her with the back of his hand. It was half a caress, half an endorsement, an admiring, desirous, newly invented touch. "Some things never go out of style," he said.

Women possess a code, a language of gesture and muscle set, which is employed when words will fail. Resorting to this, Marion issued a demure promise. *I'll give it one more try,* she confided, nodding her head against his arm, resting it there briefly.

He answered in kind, pressing his palm lightly to her cheek.

"Let's eat," she said, cropping the moment.

"Good idea," he echoed. "I'm starving."

"Did you have any trouble with the fog this morning, Clarence, coming out here?"

Compacted by the humidity, the chef's voice rang even more nasal than usual; he almost brayed. "There WERE patches here and THERE, Mrs. Falk, but nothing unmanageable. We're pretty used to these types of days up here."

"I didn't notice any instruments in you boat," Adam submitted concernedly.

Clarence was fussing with the angle of the stems in the centerpiece. Coffee and juice had been poured; the breakfast loaf was on the table. With no hint of humility, he replied, "No, sir. I don't need them."

Marion decided to pursue a different tack. "Clarence?"

"Yes, ma'am?"

While considering how to pose her question, she pinched off a thimbleful of bread and placed it in her mouth. "I wanted to ask you"— she broke off, having lost her train of thought. She had intended to probe more of the droll little man's biography, to elicit a spectrum of disclosures; yet now, suddenly, as if through received wisdom, she understood that there would be little purpose in this. Clarence, she saw, was merely an impresario; his personal history was not germane to the script. Yet somehow, through him, a story was being told, a narrative of unsuspected import, of overarching scope.

"Marion?" On his wife's face Adam beheld a novel, serene expression.

"Sorry.... I guess I drifted off.... Try the bread, dear. I'm sure you've never had anything quite like it."

And indeed he hadn't. What he experienced was beyond the sum of texture and taste. It was wholeness and plenitude, a riot of nutrients, all that grain can yield.

"Dearest?"

"Yes?"

"I feel restless. Shall we get some exercise?"

He recognized this tone: bouncy, enthused, insistent. It was the voice she had once used to lure him away from his books; with it she had lured him into chilly romps along the Charles, impromptu visits to Fenway. He had presumed he would not hear it again, that they had lost the knack of spontaneity. "Isn't that funny," he said. "I was about to make the same suggestion myself."

"Really?"

"Yes. For some reason I'm full of energy."

Their conversation fluxed through the porch screen. Inside, Marion was working a crossword puzzle; outside, Adam sat idle, perched on a rock.

"I saw a double kayak in the stacks," she said. "This is the day for it—no wind." Arising from her small, neat figure, emanating out of a partial chiaroscuro, her words sounded crisp, parting the sultry air. Still a Midwesterner, she articulated well.

"I'm game. My arms could use the toning."

"Then that's our plan."

Half an hour later they were at the dock, fully provisioned, set to go. She wore an indigo one-piece and, over it, khaki shorts; his costume effected the lifeguard: dark sunglasses, café-au-lait sweater, red trunks. As a couple they had always been quietly stylish in their athleticism.

"It looks seaworthy," Adam appraised, running his hand over the craft's inverted hull. "Fiber glass stands up well. Let's get it in the water."

They hoisted the kayak out of the rack and over their heads and carried it down to the chosen launch point, a recess in the shoreline accommodatingly matted with rockweed. Marion selected paddles and life jackets from the equipment shed while Adam cleared the cockpit of cobwebs and pine needles. They completed these tasks without offering direction to each other, as if engaged in a familiar routine. For Marion, this unspoken cooperation brought back images of the summer they had spent repainting their first domicile, a modest Tudor in Brookline; in lieu of three month's rent their live-in landlords, a Unitarian minister and his bookish wife, had accepted their labor. By the project's end they had learned to toil interconnectedly, scraping and sanding and slathering in desultory, yet amicable rhythms.

"I'll hold it while you get in," Adam offered when the knapsacks had been stowed, and the boat had been launched. In the shallow water they both struggled for footing on a mossy bottom cobbled with tide-polished stones.

"How about you?"

"I'll manage." He braced the kayak and watched her position herself, then wriggle into the bow seat; she was so quick about it that her legs seemed to have been suddenly subtracted from her, as if by the whim of some prankish cartoonist. Next, employing proper technique—paddle behind him, cantilevered off the back of the cockpit—he inserted himself into the stern.

"That was well done, dear."

"Nothing to it," he postured. "There must be a little Native American in my blood."

Craning, she turned and looked at him, confirming his presence aboard; in his life vest, propped stiffly upright, he resembled a chubby figurine in a child's pull-toy. "Okay, Hiawatha, where are we going?"

"The beach."

"The beach?"

"I've studied the map. There's a sandy strip on the southern shore of Signet Island; it should be about four miles from here."

A week or a month before, she would have doubted the wisdom of a passage over open water, the sea here so cold, so deadly; yet today she felt entirely secure, protected from harm by providential agency, by Neptune and the Nereids. "Ooo," she cooed, "that sounds lovely. We can take a dip when we get there."

Their destination decided, they set out, slipping past the breakwaters with what seemed only a few languorous strokes. The Bay was calm, a tranquil vastness textured by low, broad swells and a loose mosaic of ripples: force one. Even without a breeze the air over the water was cool; moving through it they felt refreshed, replenished. The course they followed was elliptical, first looping west toward Deer Isle, then back northeast through a cluster of small, uninhabited islands. At intervals Adam confirmed their position on a handheld G.P.S.

"We should buy ourselves one of these boats when we get back," Marion chimed, without breaking form, a couple of miles en route. "It's such a peaceful way to explore."

"I agree. I'm surprised at how much I'm enjoying this." The *this*, he realized, was not simply the outdoorsy quality of the experience, the physicality of pulling themselves across expanses of water; just as much, it was the sense of forming a mechanical unit with his wife, of pairing his motions to hers, stroking in time. Pleasantly, he was reminded of the getaway weekend they had taken to Block Island after Sarah was born: there they had dared to ride a moped double, confident that—as in the rhythms of their lovemaking—they could anticipate and move as one. "At home," he added, "we should get off our derrieres more often."

As carpenters remodel houses, so couples recoup marriages. Theirs had been nearly a teardown; aging and ill-maintained, it had needed to be stripped down to the studs to reveal that which was still salvageable, an intact and useable frame. Until recently they had doubted any possibility of reclamation; now they were confronted with clean wood, a solid basis.

"I'd like that," she sang out, making sure he could hear. "Will you take walks with me?"

And here the material to be used: for a dwelling, plaster and lath; for a relationship, specific concessions, voluntary revisions of habit.

Early in their union, oblivious to its importance in tempering their bond, he had declined to engage in the routine of an evening stroll. This refusal, through its aftermath, had enforced the lesson that women simply turn to other women when men disappoint: wherever they had lived she had spent countless hours afoot with neighbors' wives, hours slightingly deducted from the total available to him. "Of course," he answered, pretending nonchalance.

"In that case, I'll do something for you."

"What?"

"I'll try SCUBA again."

"Really?"

Their first dive trip, she had made him vow after it was over, would positively be their last. Even now the memory of it sparked chagrin, a pained awareness of his potential for thoughtlessness. One slushy February they had jetted down to Grand Cayman, *sans enfants,* for a needed reprieve. On plan, he had wheedled her into taking a beginner's course: two days in the pool, then a shallow venture from shore, and finally, an open water dive. She had fared well initially, learning to don and manipulate the cumbersome apparatus, how to balance her weight and breathe in a slow, unhurried cadence, and she had aced the paperwork, the sequential mathematics of compression and decompression; from this he had judged her ready to join him and the others—a multinational hodgepodge of Texans, Brits, and Germans—in the climactic event, a sixty-foot straight descent, to the site of a sunken trawler. But what he had neglected to factor in, yet should have, was her lifelong fear of utter darkness, exposure to things unseen. Peering down from the boat she had looked into an inky Hell, and felt the totality of panic. Despite the instructor's reassurances and his own ill-timed goads, she had remained frozen at the gunwale, the only one who balked.

"We'll hire a private guide," he promised.

We are sustained in our pairings not just by what they offer us today, but, equally, by what we project for them, the shape and texture we expect them to acquire. In marrying him, Marion had known that Adam would require aging, time in the barrel to reach maturity. Taking empathy and thoughtfulness as measures of this, she judged the process to be bearing fruit. "That would help," she said.

"I *do* try to learn from my mistakes."

"Knowing that makes them easier to forgive."

Content with these terms, this amicably redrafted paragraph within the marital bylaws, they paddled in silence for a time. Ahead of them a pair of harbor seals bobbed in and out of view. Although they gained no ground on these jolly creatures, they did on their destination; ahead of them they began to discern a slim, flesh-colored crescent, the underbelly of a green dromedary.

"It looks deserted," Marion said, when they had drawn to within half a mile.

"There's a larger beach on the other side; the tourists all go there."

"Except us?"

"We're adventurers, darling. We scorn the beaten path."

She remembered this man, her cocksure collegian, her Quixote. The one who had dreamed and dared. *Welcome back.* Merrily, she asked, "Is that our new motto? I like it."

With adolescent verve, they sprinted the rest of the way to the island, power-stroking in crisp sync. In their preoccupation with this exertion, however, they failed to observe a curiosity of the upper atmosphere, a meteorological fluke: high above them, a solitary cirrus cloud bending so far back on itself that, just briefly, it appeared to form a ring.

"Land Ho!" Marion cried mock-heroically when they touched ashore. A sand-clay mix, the beach was not the inviting, flaxen color they were used to from the Cape, but rather a drab, slightly bluish beige; unlike the assiduously raked playgrounds they had frequented further south, this coast was wrack-strewn and littered with shells. Though they tried to tiptoe across it, their footfalls crunched more often than not until they reached a less cluttered zone near the tree line.

"Some scout you are," Adam chided as they sat down to rest. "I though you said we'd have this place to ourselves."

Perplexed, Marion looked left and right. They were in a granite-bound cove which spanned no more than fifty yards. A mile away, across a bay which cut deeply into the island's southern contour, a cluster of cottages hugged a low hillside. Their part of the shoreline, by contrast, was undeveloped; there was not a soul in sight. "We do," she insisted.

"I beg to differ. We're sharing it with thousands of mollusks."

"They're quiet enough. I doubt they'll give us any trouble."

"I wouldn't be so sure."

"Oh?"

"They're all mouth. They might gossip."

It was a game: bandy the image. "Well, dear, we'll just tell them to clam up."

"That will only work with the males. If there's a truism that applies across all species, it's that you can't trust the women not to talk."

Out of the corner of his eye he saw her preparing a swat, but before she could land it he was up, chortling, warily backpedaling, inviting the chase. As she rose to follow, her face sported an eager, prankish grin, approval of their mischief. The pursuit was clumsy and comic and brief. When she overtook him they seized hold of each other, reflexively, for balance. He allowed her her recompense, let her tug scoldingly at his ears, but then, after, did what was overdue and sorely desired and entirely right: he drew her to himself. In reply, her lips—at first unresisting, then limp, then softly conforming—echoed the conclusion that he had also reached: the Falks, as a couple, could be rebuilt.

Do you remember that one pivotal kiss? Not the initial, pubescent let's-teach each-other-something, but the unique, vertiginous moment when you first tasted the ripeness, the ready, moistened flesh of your beloved? There is a form of unrest, a vibrato within the soul, that starts then; it is the watermark of romance, the heart's kinetic trace. As they embarked on their return, paddling absent-mindedly through that halcyon seascape, the Falks lapsed again into this condition, suffered an exquisite and lingering shortwindedness, a thrilling agitation.

Worse, they felt acutely unsure of themselves, tentative and ill-at-ease; on the up slope of middle age, they reprised a callow awkwardness.

When they were well offshore, Adam laid his paddle up and asked, "How are you holding up?"

"Fine, I think. I don't seem to be getting sore at all."

"I'm not either. Stonington wouldn't be that much out of the way. The guidebook describes it as a nice little village. Should we make a detour?"

Marion gauged her energy to be undiminished, possibly even enhanced; within the atmosphere she felt a charge, a teeming, a welling of ions. "It's still early," she said. "We can look around for knickknacks."

Thus in accord, they turned northwesterly, further up the Bay. By now the sea breeze was up, darkening and corrugating the surface of the water. Coming out to meet it, they observed a steady procession of vessels—day-sailors bound for Vinalhaven or Isle au Haut—filtering down the eastern passage; even on a weekday, it appeared, these sapphire reaches were too much the playground for many to resist.

"I have something funny to ask you," Adam announced during the next rest.

Three days earlier she might have tried to deflect him, afraid of having to field some recriminative inquiry, but not now. "Go ahead."

"Do you feel....vague?"

"How do you mean?"

He scanned the lower altitudes for the words to continue with. "I wish I could explain it well. I have this odd sensation, like there's a fog at the center of my mind."

Marion balanced her paddle on the hull and lowered her hands over the sides, trailing her fingers in the water. After a moment of deliberation, she admitted, "I think I've been experiencing something similar."

Still gliding, the kayak tapped gently against the waves.

"You have?"

"It doesn't bother me, though; it's a pleasant kind of vagueness. It's the way I used to feel sometimes, waking up after a great party: content, but a little fuzzy-headed."

"Precisely."

"What do you think it is?"

"I don't know. I can't bring myself to worry about it, though."

"I can't either. Right now, actually, I find it hard to worry about anything."

In Stonington they tied up to the main floating dock and ascended a ladder to the pier above. After three days of near-solitude this seasonally vibrant town, thronged with yacht owners and tourists, hobbyists and fishermen, was almost too urban for them; more than they could have expected, their temperaments had been reset by the emollient rhythms of the outer islands, the lulling constancy of wind and wave. A short walk inland brought them to the principal avenue of commerce, predictably named "Main Street."

"How odd!" Marion declared, stopping at a curb. "I definitely feel like I've seen this place before."

"You probably have, in a travel book. It's the quintessential seaside village."

A dense, trite panorama loomed in their view: clapboard storefronts and gilt-lettered signs, scrofulous street artists and doddering retirees.

"But it's strange to actually *be* here," she amplified. "You never think spots like this actually exist. It's so Norman Rockwell."

Adam turned full-face to the early afternoon sun and closed his eyes long enough to feel its heat, its radiated blessings, settling upon his lids; when he opened them again he seemed to look out upon a world from which, obscurely, some set of taints had been removed. "Let's explore the canvas," he proposed, taking her hand.

For the next hour they toured the town, combing through antique shops, souvenir mills, camping outfitters, even real estate offices. And if they refrained from making purchases in these places, it was perhaps out of the conviction that the removal of any item would constitute a desecration, a plucking at a scene rendered in gingerbread; they were more than content just to window-shop, to peruse historical legends, to roam about with the hordes.

Toward the end of their saunter, as they paused in front of a gallery featuring marine art, Marion, at last, posed the inevitable question: "What's happening to us, Adam?"

He studied their reflections in the glass, two translucent busts superimposed on the compositions within. Could these be those same figures they used to observe, on golden-bright autumn days, in the display cases along Newbury Street? As newlyweds they had been content to live in the hypothetical, making imaginary purchases for their future home. "I'm not sure," he said, "but I'm not going to second-guess it."

"I feel like we're dating, like we don't have a history together."

"We seem new, don't we?"

"What are we supposed to do at this point?"

A week ago, he recalled, she had been beyond taking his advice. "We take our time," he said. "We see what comes."

"We did that before, didn't we?"

"Twenty-odd years ago."

Resolutely, she squeezed his hand and said, "We can do it again, I'm sure."

And in this sweetly dazed and expectant mind frame they made their way back to the dock, cognizant that they were again a work-in-progress, a man and a woman recurving in time.

The wind had firmed by the time they pushed off; a mild chop now scalloped the surface of the Bay.

"I still don't feel tired," Marion boasted halfway back to their island. To the contrary, her body felt lighter, freer, like a mechanism which, through its own motion, dispels the viscosity surrounding its parts.

"Your muscles are warmed up. You'll feel them in the morning; I'll guarantee it."

Granting his point, she admitted, "They're underused, I'm afraid." In the last five or six years she had become more and more sedentary, and at the margins, contentedly lazy. She had no regimen, no personal trainer; self-deceptively, she had permitted her twice-weekly doubles games to count as an exercise program. "Will you jog with me sometimes?"

Adam had long considered all couples who ran together, particularly those in matching Dacron, hopelessly gauche. They struck him as too overtly wholesome, too bound by appearances, to be anything but laughable. Fitness, in his book, was a condition to be achieved through private rigors, without needless adornments. From underneath, however, arising from some musky recess of his being, a surprise pulse of androgen pushed aside this censoriousness. He pictured predators copulating after the hunt; he imagined these same couples having sweaty sex before turning on the shower. "I will," he heard himself say.

"Then I'll go skiing again." Her offer was spoken slowly, avowedly. Among their previously shared athletic pursuits, this had been her last withhold.

"Truly?"

At her peak she had been a companionable skier, good enough to ride any lift and find a negotiable, if often indirect, line of descent. Yet as her skills had improved, so had his tendency to leverage them; though he had once skied in tandem with her, letting her lead, he had begun to range ahead, beckoning her onto steeper slopes, more undulant terrain. When the inevitable mishaps occurred—pitch-poling falls off moguls, leg-splaying wipeouts in the powder—he had foolishly played the martinet, urging perseverance, unyielding resolve; perceiving that she was becoming the victim of overzealous instruction, fearing in her husband the taskmaster she had known in her father, she had opted out, hung up the slats. "But you have to take me out West," she qualified. "No more *ice.*"

"We should try Utah; it's supposed to have the best snow."

"Or Tahoe. We can look at the lake as we schuss along."

A modest but credible version of their future now scrolled through Adam's mind. It would be good enough just like this. They did not have to reclaim a steaming passion for each other; they could be happy without being love-struck. What was important—what they still had—was friendship. It had taken this trip for hem to establish that.

"Marion—"

"Yes?"

"You're my chum."

In a trough she completed a long, determined stroke, spinning the brine into a tight eddy. "And you're mine, Adam."

"I don't really need anything more from you."

"And from you, my sweet, I would have nothing less."

In the interval it would take him to digest her affirmation, Marion caught a last glimpse of what might have been: an abode at least temporarily uncluttered by male debris, a household fitted entirely to her tastes, rooms of her own. This much she forfeited now. "Adam," she pledged, "I'll stay."

What we value most in our players, the stars of stage and screen, is their ability to render the moment, to interpret it greatly. Had we all this knack, a here's-looking-at-you-kid kind of style, we should need fewer Bogarts, for we ourselves would be larger than life. But the Falks, in this respect, were only middling, neither talented nor inept at conveying sentiment, and thus to the extent that this scene between them was carried off imperfectly, they would afterwards seek to see it recreated, to be treated by Broadway and Hollywood to a bolder, more storied version of themselves.

"I would like that very much."

"Are you sure?"

"I'm sure."

"There are plenty of other women out there, dear; I can't do this again, I can't lose you twice."

"You didn't lose me a first time."

"I did, almost. We were almost there: separated."

Finessing a stroke, he suggested a consolation. "Perhaps it was something we had to go through, so we could come out okay."

"Like surgery, or chemo?"

"A period of repair, let's call it."

Unanswered, his words hung in the air: coalescing, turning upper case. Yes: REPAIR. Assenting to it in silence, they deemed this a suitable caption for the process they had fallen into in these recent, extraordinary days. Then, as if to usher it forward, to facilitate its work, they returned their attention to the details of nature. Marion studied the flight of a distant cormorant; Adam watched the bow waves form and dissipate. But a pity it was that they were not able to peer down into the depths they were traversing, for within them they would have witnessed a marvel: large schools of grunts and snappers and other species of fish not customarily found in that region.

Back on the island, they pursued a digressive route up to the house; unhindered by rancor, their spirits led them askance, inveigling them to see all the local verdure. Here and there they paused to cull hawkweed, pick blueberries, sample the fragrance of goldenrod; with scientific inquisitiveness they studied the patterning of lichen, tested the springiness of mosses; invested with a newfound attentiveness, they perused the spare, tenacious flora of that northerly realm. It was a leisurely, informative perambulation, a poignant revival of their habit of exploring the botanic gardens of new and unfamiliar cities. Now, however, wherever they looked, they seemed to see more; their perceptions were keener. Take the cinquefoil: previously they would have noticed just the tiny, curling white petals and the yellow disc— the flower alone; now they also observed calyx and stalk, anther and ovary; now they divined the labor of chloroplasts, the exodus of oxygen from the leaves. Now they witnessed the complexity, beheld the wonder.

When they convened to examine a bayberry, Adam tried to express it: "Is this what Outward Bound does to you?"

"What?"

"I feel like my mind has opened up to itself, like I'm practicing Zen."

Marion parted one branch from the rest, holding it in relief against her palm. "It's what they call an 'aha!' moment," she said. With her free hand, she fingered a cluster of the fruit, confirming its waxy texture. "The remarkable thing—"

"Yes?"

"The remarkable thing is that I believe I've entered it with you."

"So much the better; this is something we *should* share."

They had never been here before, they realized; this experience was entirely new. Even in their headiest days they had never suspected that their consciousnesses could overlap; no less than any other couple, their conjointness had always stopped at the border of subjectivity. But at this instant a common door seemed to have opened between their two beings, and in some rooms their thoughts had intermingled. "What it shows," she said, "is that we've found peace with each other."

He checked the impulse to take her in his arms, to undress and ravish her, to reconsummate their union. Their physical rapprochement, he knew, would come soon enough. It was better this other way: first they would become lovers incorporeally, baring not the body but the soul. "We've been seeking it so long," he said.

Releasing the shrub, Marion moved two or three steps up to higher ground. There she turned her face to the breeze and the westering sun. And in the soft, warm pressure which their combination exerted against it she felt the work of an undeciphered force, what it was that was saving them.

Thayer Street, named, as are many of the thoroughfares in Providence, after a beneficent nineteenth century textile baron, is a tidy, commercially-zoned concourse which hems Brown University on the east. During the academic year its sidewalks brim with collegians of all stripes: prankish undergrads, tweedy profs, supercilious T.A.'s. In the mid-afternoons and throughout the weekends, small bands of neighborhood adolescents, shirking adult supervision, filter into the mix. Though diverse, it is a population which is, on the whole, affluent, educated, law-abiding. Knowledgeable of this, the city police post only a token presence, leaving the pursuit of the occasional purse-snatcher to the campus gendarmes, an unarmed ersatz squad clad in the school sepia and scarlet. Come summer, however, the students disperse, the faculty retreats from view, and most of the pimply interlopers repair with their parents to the beach, to Westport or Weekapaug or Watch Hill. But nature, as it is said, abhors a vacuum, and hence, to the pavements thus bared, there is an advent of an entirely different crowd. By Harley and window-shaded van they arrive, a brazen ruck, tattooed legions of dopers and con-men, vagrants and roustabouts. In the cafés the talk turns from heroines to heroin; on the corners polemicism defaults to pugilism. Inexorably, the place takes on the atmosphere of a carnival, and it is only a generous deployment of Providence's finest, hip-booted regulars afoot and on horseback, which stanches a progression into anarchy. Still, at the least, it is a noisy, rough-and-tumble scene, a chancrous eruption on the countenance of civility.

Had she been trying to wend her way alone through this melee, Sarah Falk might have felt vulnerable. No telling, after all, when someone in this leather-braceleted crowd might try for an ass-grab, a scurrilous little pinch. But tonight—thank goodness—she had Carl at her side; in his escort she felt championed, secure. Six-three and broad-shouldered, the center on his high-school football team, he was a far cry from the willowy, intellectual type she had imagined herself with, in a passel of maidenly dreams, during the first months after her arrival. From Maryland, a letter-carrier's son, she had met him four months ago in statistics lab. From the beginning they had known that their match-up was anomalous, an outlier: blue-collar-boy-hoping-to-make-it-big-in-business-meets-career-confused-daughter-of-privilege. The currents of passion, however, do not pause for a reckoning of complementarities, and within one heated, damn-the-classes winter week, they had become an item, alias swain and shepherdess, Daphnis and Chloe. Both juniors next year, they had opted for the off-campus prerogative, and now, unbeknownst to their parents, they were out to make good on it. "Which one did you like best?" she asked, a jounce in her step, swinging their linked hands widely forward.

They were passing a marquee. Scanning this, as if to discern his answer, the boy replied, "The loft, I think. I like having the bedroom on the second floor."

She harvested his meaning: even with friends over, they could sneak upstairs for a quickie. His concupiscence did her proud. "It's halfway down the Hill," she reminded him. "The climb won't bother you?" During the day they had looked at half a dozen apartments; the one under discussion was well beneath the bluff from which John Nicholas Brown had watched his slavers pulling into port, tucked away in a declivitous little alley that had been the bane of generations of skateboarders, roller-bladers, and extreme sportsmen.

"It will be good for us—good for those gorgeous legs of yours."

Commingled with his lust, he exhibited an attitude of proprietorship which was new to her. Her other liaisons had taught her that she was desirable, that her fine-boned, small-breasted physique was an aesthetically and sexually acceptable variety—one, albeit, of many—but he had been the first to demonstrate an intent to secure it, invest in it, safeguard it for future use. "I like it, too!" she chirped, spinning on tiptoe. "Then it's settled! We have our first place together!"

"Ours!" the boy echoed nonchalantly, high-fiving her. "Let's celebrate over—" ahead, his eye seized on a sign upholding a cluster of multicolored orbs—"over ice cream."

As far as there are commonalities of appearance among new and still deepening romances, Carl and Sarah presently illustrated every one. Arm-over-arm, their heads inclined together, they proceeded up the street in the guise of an unsteady, sheepishly giggling, four-legged creature: Love's apparition. Organically, they seemed one entity, one being, and when they separated again to enter the shop, it was as if they had each hatched, one from the other.

"Let's sit," Sarah prompted, noticing that a table next to the window was free.

Circumventing the crowd milling around the freezer cases, they quickly ensconced themselves. Though dusk was gathering, an enervating heat still hung over the city; it was a relief to have found repose in this cooler, pleasantly fragrant spot. "That's more like it," Carl extolled, stretching out his legs. "I could be happy here for quite a while."

Seated more at his side than across from him, Sarah gathered a profile view of her young man, her catch. From this perspective he looked classically Roman: the squat nose, the prominent eyes, the short thick curls. He was practically in the net now, wasn't he? In two short weeks they would be—eeek!—cohabitating. The fact seemed to have crept up on her. Very soon she would be—what?—spoken for? Off the market? And from there it might only be a hop-skip-and-a-jump to being banded, wedded, kept. Before it was too late it behooved her to parse the downside, envision the risks.

She did not have to look far.

Her parents, she knew, had been unhappy for years. They did not fight openly, and neither one had chosen to reveal his or her stigmata to her, but signs of their disharmony had long been evident. Her mother was given to protracted intervals of staring into empty vistas and retreating to empty rooms; her father conveyed his distress more audibly, through a phlegmy repertoire of lugubrious exhalations. In each other's company they appeared either wary or indifferent, freshly wounded or sealed off behind old scars. To give herself pause, she thought, it would be sufficient to conjure up a vignette, a representative sample of their interaction. So, an exercise. In the halls of her imagination she erected a set, crafted a diorama. For the mise en scene—just as here—she employed two chairs and a table, dubbing in the sounds, the scents, of the seacoast. By her watch it was eight o'clock: they would be having dinner at about this time. (She had forgotten exactly where in Maine they were, but presumed there must be a clam shack in the vicinity.) She pictured them awaiting service, in that diagnostic interval before food becomes available to occupy, to distract. Then, from the vantage point of an eavesdropper, she let the action roll:

I want you to promise me one thing, she heard her father say. As he spoke he leaned in, preparing to speak the next words in confidence.

What is it? came the reply.

This was not the scene she had anticipated. On her mother's face she saw a balmy expression, a rosy contentedness. She had the look of a person to whom something long yearned-for had been granted.

You won't change your mind.

Tenderly yet emphatically, in the manner of a lover exchanging a troth, she saw her mother reach out and grasp her father's hand. *Why would I? This is going to be wonderful for both of us.*

Her father's voice thickened. *I know it is. It will make us even closer.*

What trick was this? Sarah wondered, snuffing the reverie. She had thought dreams were the province of invention, but now her conscious mind, too, was trafficking in fiction. For there was no verisimilitude in this little skit. How implausible, the notion that her parents' romance could be rekindled by some fond project, some affecting endeavor! Wishful thinking, this could only be. *Well, enough of that,* she mused, turning to see the menu board. Better to consider something edible and flavorful. Something actual. Something real.

"This is great! When was the last time we did something like this?"

Uplifted, Marion's gaze panned the constellations, the vast, gossamer ornamentation suspended in the dome of night. Amidst this pantheon, she recognized only three groups by name: the two Dippers and Orion. When they got back home, she resolved, she must find a course, acquire a dilettantish knowledge of astronomy. "I think it was in Vermont," she recalled, "after we dropped David off that summer. Remember?"

Adam traced the clue back nearly a decade, to a riverside grove. They had enrolled their son in a camp in the Green Mountains, arriving late and lingering through dinner. Fatigue had overtaken them on the way back, and they had stopped along Otter Creek at dusk, intending to just nap; yet the site that they had happened upon had proven so inviting, so idyllic, that they had spent the night instead, snugly cocooned in a picnic blanket. "We're better equipped this time," he observed, "thanks to you."

Marion's irrepressible curiosity, her resolute delving into every dusty drawer and closet, every naphthalened compartment in the house, had led her, up a pull-down stairway, to a small attic where winter outerwear and camping equipment were stored. Here she had discovered sleeping bags and mattresses and trail pillows, all that was needed for an evening *en plain air.* "I don't think they would mind us using this stuff," she ventured, leaving in her tone a strand of hesitancy, a nod towards negotiability, which invited him to vet the issue: if this marriage of theirs were to be resurrected, she could no longer discount his point of view.

"You're probably right. I would have felt better if we had met them and asked them specifically, though."

Above them, poised beyond the inky troposphere, behind the twinkling scrim of the galaxy, Marion inferred the presence of a watchful power, a reticent beneficence which guided her, healingly, to say, "Perhaps we can—next year."

Adam had been lying supine; pivoting onto one elbow, he made out his wife's silhouette, her high forehead and plummy cheeks, offset against the lustrous northern sea. They were situated at the highest elevation on the island, facing eastward. "How?"

"They live in Philadelphia. If they drive up the coast to get here, they can stay with us for a night; we're just over halfway."

It was possible; likely, even. She had made a clutch of friends— for herself, for them—by transcending the New England ethos: the stubborn insularity, the terse standoffishness. Their address book was replete with amities culled from sidelines and waiting rooms, beach resorts and barstools. Socially, he had grown fat on this sustenance. "I like that idea," he emphasized.

Bustling within the layers of nylon that enveloped them— felicitously, they had found two identical bags that could be zipped together—Marion sidled closer to him, into the spooning position. She had missed their pillow talks, the earnest desultory confessions they made to each other before sleep. Without them her spirit had become doubly burdened; she had found no other way to expurgate the inexorable weedy growth of petty grievances that cluttered her soul. "I'm dying to see what they're like," she admitted. "I've been studying their pictures, as you know. The wife looks like the kind of person who grew up on a farm."

"And the husband?" He had known this analysis was in the offing. After cocktail parties she would offer detailed exegeses of people she had barely met.

"Oh, he's the financial type. He's more urbane but less approachable."

"Too much of a prig, is he?"

"Actually, not. He can seem stuck up at first, but once you get to know him he's actually very decent." She paused, considered, and then carefully said, "He's quite a bit like you."

"Ah."

They kept bumping into words that distilled, that clarified. First, REPAIR. Now, DECENT. With singular efficiency it reacted within her consciousness, shocking out the cloudiness, setting her husband's character in clear view. Her voice slipped half an octave: "I picked you because you're a good person, Adam."

His hand found the back of her neck, the soft skin there a proxy for all the other parts of her. For now, he resolved, he would let it be such. He would proceed no further in caressing this form, these curves that he knew. In effecting reserve he would pay her respect, what any gentleman owes in the beginning. He would take her later, yes, but only reluctantly—reverently—as if it were the first time. "And all along," he quipped, "I thought it was the pedigree."

"That was just a bonus."

"If only I had been so pure. I saw nothing but dollar signs from the moment I met you."

"I know, my mother tried to warn me—"

"But I was a determined gold digger; I wouldn't let you go."

It was a form of closure to joke about money. With the kids gone, the divorce would have been about nothing else: *beaucoup* high-priced haggling over premarital property, commingled assets, equitable distribution. They knew many couples who had been severely shriven in the process, a few for whom it never seemed to end.

"It's not my fault for being an inheritee," Marion declared. She sounded, at last, convinced of it.

"And it's not my fault for marrying one."

"Those are two hang-ups we can do without."

"Here, here! Good riddance to neurotic guilt!"

Marion squirmed like a child relishing a scheme. She told him, "We need to prove to ourselves that we're really rid of it. We have to splurge on something."

"Do you have anything in mind?"

"Something we can both use—a hot tub, if we can figure out where to put it."

Adam conceived a tidy project on their second floor. On an amateur blueprint he drew trusses and housings, and over them, an octagonal platform. With guidance from the contractor, he might even take a stab at some of the carpentry. "We can rework that little upper deck we never use," he explained. "If we cut a door out to it from the bathroom we can come and go as we please."

Enticed by this promise of more laid-back living, a Californian ease, Marion tucked herself firmly into the arc of Adam's body. Dreamily she transposed them, still fitted front-to-back, into a bubbling azure crucible. She pictured them with drinks in-hand, heads back, listening to a Coltrane or Stan Getz riff; above them, much as this one, the sky was populous with stars, a canopy of portents she had at last learned to interpret. She would be ready for him then, ready to submit eagerly—and often—to his overtures; she was ready now. "The heat will be good for our joints as we get older," she predicted.

"It will give us an excuse to be outside at night," he added, "the way we are here."

"And it will be twice the fun."

"Why?"

"We won't be wearing any clothes, silly."

The late news, again, was mostly mayhem. Gang wars, narcotic slayings, random fracases. In a city the size of Chicago there was never a dearth of violence; scenes of carnage burbled up in abundance through the editing rooms, into the broadcast booths. *Just once,* thought Julia Scott, *they should limit themselves to stories about good deeds, peaceableness, some human progress. Now* that *would be news.*

Admittedly, it was not a desire to learn the events of the just-passed day that made her a viewer. Rather, her interest was entirely in the coming one. To a degree that had become ritualistic, she loved to watch the weather. Every evening, to be granted a preview—even if only meteorological—of the approaching morning seemed to augment her chances of actually reaching it. For she had reached that stage of agedness where one counts the minutes, the hours, as they pass as small victories, territories wrested from a murky borderland, temporal extensions of the self.

She had long thought of dying as a stillness, a calm. It gathered around you insidiously, like a fog; it lifted away your capacity for sensation, for responsiveness. Yet what her quietus might entrain behind this leading edge she puzzled at. Was it an event or a process? A point or a continuum? What frightened her was the possibility that death, as much as life, was a state of being, something ongoing. During the day, she kept busied enough to eschew these questions. Narrowed though it was by senescence, her agenda was still crowded by tea parties and bridge groups and ladies' luncheons: all the falderal of a Lake Forest widow. No, pointedly, it was the nights she feared, especially the dread interval, never brief, between when she switched off the television and the bedside lamp and when sleep bestowed its mercies upon her. Inevitably, during those leaden minutes, she pondered the parameters—the subjectivity—of her continuance: what the hereafter would hold for her. And though she tried gamely to see it otherwise, to muster a vision of palm fronds and turquoise seas, her mind insisted on displaying ashen versions of Limbo, dreary nether realms where she and other departeds drifted as dust, voiceless debris in a gray nothingness. She had attempted to peer through these spaces to discover boundaries, thresholds—some hope of salvation— but to no avail; they appeared limitless, infinitely capacious, volumes without dimension. By default, her recourse had been pharmacological, a generous dose of sedative. She could feel it hitting her now: with the medicine in her she was more numb, more stoical. And though it seemed like cheating, she was happy to have at least this partial antidote to her apprehensiveness, her septuagenarian's angst.

The weatherman was young, Hispanic, homosexual; his name was Ramon Hernandez. They were working him in as a successor to the mainstay, a jowly yet affable man who, in recent years, had started to resemble her neighbor's basset hound. Perhaps a residue of dance training, Ramon had a swiveling, toe-pointing style of moving around the set, and his routine incorporated an assortment of hand flourishes and other effeminacies. Tomorrow, he foretold, would be "boffo:" blue skies with low humidity; the weekend looked a bit more iffy: a possibility of afternoon showers, small craft warnings on the Lake. However it turned, the outlook was for vivid weather, energizing conditions. People did not succumb on such days, Julia assured herself; they died when the skies were insipidly hazy or overcast. In her declining days she had embraced certain fallacies as balms.

"Well enough," she muttered as the segment ended. She clicked the remote and, rolling on her side, found the toggle switch on the lamp cord. Abruptly, the dark loomed. Resignedly, she waited for her adumbrations to return, taking shape against the ceiling's insufficient opaqueness. Outside, under the cover of ancient oaks and elms, the suburban wilds swelled with activity; through a window screen she heard a chorus of cicadas, the circumambient gossip of countless small creatures. There was comfort available in this commotion, she had previously decided; within it the energy sustaining the world became tangible, extant. The Earth remained potent: here was audible proof. Long after her time it would continue to fashion corollas out of dull matter. Yet by what inspiration? What ingenuity was it that so artfully directed nature's work? For certainly the gratuitous beauty of the aster or the tulip exceeded the requirements, the logic, of evolution. Unaided, mere genes could not craft such glory. But if a flower be the product of some designedness beyond itself, then from whence?

How strange it was, she thought, that she should be considering these questions, and so belatedly! She had always been a staunch agnostic; she had never been swayed by the propositions of religion. To her all faiths were, as in Marx's dictum, opiates. She maintained a high regard for those who, like herself, abstained, and she abhorred the "foxhole Christians," the craven ones who, at the last minute, caved. Far better to go out with your principals intact. Yet it must be granted that there was virtue in open-mindedness. Too, she was aware that many top scientists, unable to solve the mysteries within their purview, became believers in the end. Thus, the question: if the Divine could be apprehended in subatomic structures and quantum phenomena was it any less so in the wonders to be beheld in a garden?

Hardly.

On subsequent nights she would assemble gazebos and pergolas, finicky, ornate constructions conceived in her imagination and lifted into the polyhedral space above her bed; these and other forms of trelliswork would seem necessary containments for an abundance, then a superfluity, of floral expressions her mind would set there. In time every species, every variety, would be represented. Floribundas would mingle with polyanthuses, creepers would sport with climbers. Her fanciful garden would feature all manner of exotic hybrids and hues never achieved in actual cultivation. It would be a haven, a richly scented bower her spirit would enter nightly, emerging refreshed—restored—the morning after. Above all, it would be a place where she tended hope, a frail but not insubstantial convincedness that there was something yet to come, a desirable perpetuity.

But all things begin discretely; the anlage is less elaborate than its expression. Thus on this seminal night her consciousness set before itself, in a bed otherwise dormant, a single, thornless white rose. Yet from even this one plant there spread a telling radiance, a corona of goodly luminosity, the color of Grace.

FRIDAY

Lub-dub, lub-dub. Her ear not a stethoscope, but practically as good. She heard no extra sounds—what did they call them? Clicks. Rubs. Gallops. She had paid attention when he had brought her along to lectures; she had read portions of his books; she had learned enough about cardiology to beware hiccups in a rhythm, small noises out of joint. But though a heart starts or shudders as it fails, she thought, there's less commotion if it simply aches. In his she detected no altered cadence, no suspicious patter. Yet beneath this bony vault, beneath this shy nipple, she knew, there laid a wounded organ, a knot of hurt. Did sleep relieve it? *Then rest, my sweet, abide. And in the morning a poultice I'll provide. Tenderness. Constancy. Mirth. All my withheld charms. A doctor I'm not, but heal you I will.*

Brian Beirne has no partiality for the supernatural; he is not the type—and there are one or two on every dock—to peer into the fog or the moonless night and see illusory shapes, shadowy minions, phantoms. But neither does he dismiss the notion that there are occurrences in nature that leave one to puzzle at the cause, and wonder if it can be earthly. In point of fact, he is still pursuing a sensible explanation for a phenomenon he witnessed recently, while making the rounds on his lobster boat. He would like to be able to pass it off as some sort of display—mating behavior or notice of territorial infringement—but the references he has consulted, two *Field Guides* and a tome entitled *Sea Birds of the World*, have not supported such an interpretation, and his panel of experts, the half-dozen birdwatchers and charter captains whom he has queried, have hewed to a skeptical line. For now, therefore, the episode resides in abeyance in his logbook, a double-asterisked entry, the humble record of what was seen:

25 June

Early start this morning. The sky as spectacular as ever. High clouds only, pinkish dawn. Nothing better. Why I try to make a living off the sea. Of all the days to be single-handing! The first mate called in "sick" again, the lazy arse. He should have been here as my witness, seconding this account. Well, damn the sluggard! This is what he missed. On the run out, passing Matthew Island, I see a swarm of birds. Must be a school of blues chasing bait, I think at first. But then I notice that the birds aren't over water; they're over the island. And now the amazing thing: like someone has trained them, they're flying single-file around a pattern that crosses itself. Two intersecting loops. A figure eight.
The truth! I swear it!

Underneath his conscious mind, below the level of reason, Adam had achieved a feat of engineering. There, where we sometimes replay the facts of our lives, our tangled personal histories, he had erected an elaborate infrastructure, an architecture of escapism. It was, if you will, a species of duct-work, a labyrinth of chutes and tubes, spouts and spillways, that allowed him to slip back into the past and then, fictively, sideways: into the option not taken, the opportunity never pursued.

For example, the month before, aboard a train to New Haven, having lapsed into that narcotic othermindedness that travel induces, he had stepped through a portal, skittered down a silvery passageway, and elided back twenty-five years into the arms of Connie Frye. Grade school classmates, they had had a brief, circumscribed affair before going off to college: she to Pomona, he to Princeton. Knowing the distance that would soon separate them had required them to treat it as a mere dalliance, a didactic little adventure, a rehearsal for the other loves to come. But on the train that day he had imagined—emotionally relished—a different outcome. Connie had altered her plans, chosen Bryn Mawr instead; offered a chance for viability, their flirtation had rooted and blossomed. Stouter and less sharply etched than Marion, she had nevertheless made an agreeable bride: not as cosmopolitan, but generally cheerier and more reachable. In his reverie he had pictured them on the outskirts of a village in upstate New York, dandling twin toddlers, picnicking in a sweet-smelling field. Vicariously, he had experienced the complacency, the unambitious contentedness that is the backbone of marriage; fleetingly he had revisited happiness.

He had learned to slide away like this at any hour, in all varieties of circumstances: during a break between patients, while holding on the phone, in the act of pumping gas. The more dismayed he had become with the actual text of his existence, the more agility he had acquired at transposing himself into fictional alternatives. Indeed, these forays into the hypothetical, the realm of the but-for-this-or-that, had come to constitute a prop to his confidence; they had served to convince him that he had been brought low not by personal failing but by hapless choice, the short straw.

If he had a favorite time, a preferred venue in which to rework his fate, it was surely this: these inviolable minutes just as he was awakening, before the world could lay its claims on him. In this space he could reach furthest, delve most extensively, into what could have been. It had become almost a habit to start each day thus, with a modified reminiscence, some segment of his biography retouched—improved—by the application of hindsight. This morning, however, as his imagination gathered momentum, he felt it bend in a new direction. Now gravity did not seem to provide the impetus; instead, he had a sense of being lifted, of being propelled higher by a concentrated updraft; and curiously, he was unable to lay hold of the past in any respect, for it was beneath him, receding into oblivion. His mind, he realized, was looping *forward* in time. As before, he seemed to pass through an assemblage featuring many branches and outlets, points of divergence at each juncture, each date; but at the end of his transit he would be arriving, not returning. Then it struck him: this is normal, what an ordinary, reasonably contented person does—scouting the territory ahead, scanning the possibilities, believing in a few.

If they could have remembered the taste of the bread that morning—even so, could they ever have described it? For what is the aroma of new beginnings, what is the consistency of hope? And how could they have explained that through ingesting it they felt not only nourished but reset, realigned? It would have taken an uncommon articulateness, a felicity with the language, to limn the experience, to capture it in words. Just as well, whom could they have told? At best it would have seemed utter foolishness, an aspect of some folk tale or country yarn taken too literally, a beguiling inanity.

Call it a blessing, therefore—and perhaps the requirement of some unknown proviso—that the exceptional qualities of that loaf passed through their minds leaving no trace of themselves. For in seeking the source of all our bounties, we must look through a glass, darkly.

Lazily, through the juniper tint of his sunglasses, Adam surveyed the skies. Far above them a lone jet trail angled southwest, stitching its way through a raft of cirrus clouds. *Must be the early risers coming in from London or Frankfurt,* he surmised. *High rollers, international bankers. A celebrity exec, or two. Over your head, all of it. Accounting so much as Greek to you, Falk. You would have made a terrible financier. Just be content with what you are. Physician. Healer. Low-earning, but respectable. It should be enough.* Capping the thought, he turned on his side. Marion, he saw, was working on her back; they had been tanning together for almost an hour. Quizzically, he asked, "Were we really unhappy with each other recently? It doesn't seem possible."

Arms forward, Marion propped herself up on her elbows, assuming a Sphinx-like pose. In the distance she observed a schooner, its sails nearly diaphanous in the easterly light, skimming the horizon. "We were," she said, deliberating, "but now I hardly seem to know what the trouble was; it all seems so distant."

It was occurring to them both that they might be learning, somehow, to rise above the grit, the trifling disappointments and petty setbacks of married life; that they might cease accumulating frustrations and resentments; that life might actually become easy. In the warmth of the solstitial sun, they felt themselves settling further into a golden harmony, a new stage.

"Adam?"

"Yes, love?"

"When we get back, I want to de-clutter."

"Come again?"

"We have so much unneeded junk; I'd like to get rid of a lot of it."

"Nigel and Hannah can coach us; they're such minimalists." Among their more exotic friends were the Pembertons, an Anglo-Dutch couple living in the Back Bay. He was an architect, and she was a copy editor; mutually, they had embraced a lifestyle almost fanatically devoid of color and superfluity. They dressed in black and grays; they decorated ascetically. Simplicity was their mantra, and they carried it to extremes.

"I'm sorry I've kidded them about it all these years. Now I understand their aim: not being a slave to material things."

"That's what Buddhism is all about—remember? We suffer on account of our manufactured wants, our artificial desires."

Marion figured the benefits of austerity. No more aimless catalogue-combing; no more hankering after baubles. Consumerism would lose its grip. She would spend only for sustenance, functionality, altruistic purpose. "The Four Noble Truths," she recalled.

In the second half of medical school he had taken up meditation, seeking a means to quiet his mind, to repel from consciousness the day's brutal imagery: the botched intubations, failed resuscitations, gushing exsanguinations. Later, curious about the benefits of all those protracted exhalations and arcane chants, she had joined in. For a short time they had attended workshops, puzzled over koans, practiced "centering." Then came internship and babies and home ownership—an onslaught of priorities—leaving them little time to probe the frontiers of awareness. Yet even though they had had to forsake the habit, their experience with it had convinced them of the value, the moral necessity, of renouncing avarice, a dependency on objects. Adam felt himself retrieving this philosophy now; the world outside this moment, this dialogue, this relationship, should be extraneous. "We need to work on shedding things if they get in the way," he agreed.

With feline grace, effort concealed by fluidity, Marion folded back on her haunches and slowly stood, a geisha arising from the mat. A coy, mesmeric smile formed upon her lips. Her cheeks flushed. Her gaze turned moist and absolving. "Take my hand," she said, reaching down to him. "I know where we should start."

Obediently, he arced his fingers around hers. The firmness of her grip, the determination it conveyed, surprised him. She applied an upward pressure on his palm, a dancer's lead, and he, too, rose. They stood before each other, not speaking for a minute, partaking in the last of their disaffection, their ambivalence, then he asked, "Are you taking me on an expedition?"

"Only to a place you've already been."

Adroitly, she escorted him off the rocks, through the screened porch, into the living room. *Here* she decided. *On the rough carpet.* She peeled off one strap of her bathing suit, then the other, and turned to face him. She wanted, suddenly, to be abused: slapped, manhandled, punished for all the privations she had put him through, all the lapsed courtesies, curtailed attentions, snuffed-out conversations. Their estrangement, considered at its endpoint, seemed an unjust sentence she had passed on him; for this misprision she deserved chastisement, pain. "Do you still want me?" she asked.

Abstinence potentiates even the familiar. The sight of her breasts, such luscious unguarded fruit, left him dry-throated. She had not offered them to him like this—for any use, any duration, by light of day—in so long that they seemed to attach to someone else, an unknown woman, and this encounter between them, though they were man and wife, felt initiatory, virginal. "More than ever," he managed.

She drew closer and slowly, methodically, unbuttoned his shirt. Her fingers, splaying, rediscovered the shallow recesses behind his clavicles, the dense earnest masses of his shoulders. She had forgotten how informative it could be to touch him, to caress the sculptural detail which the eye overlooks. As their love had paled her psyche had made him into an abstraction, an other; it had rinsed him of physicality. Now he was acquiring sinew and bone again, becoming incarnate. "How's your neck?" she inquired, kneading the flesh above his trapezoids. Orthopedically, he was still largely intact, save for the occasional crick.

"Limber," he proclaimed. "I'll demonstrate." Angling in, he held her hair away and kissed the taut, untanned skin below her ear. From there his lips rushed on to reacquaint themselves with her upper body, her polleny, well-tended physique. Her collarbone was more prominent, and her larynx less so, than he might have gauged; the jut of her jaw was still firm and proud, but above it her cheeks had grown fuller, pulpier. "You're gorgeous," he whispered, coming up for air, "as gorgeous as ever."

She believed it: believed him because she again believed in *them*. A woman is always beautiful to the man who adores her. As to how she might be rated by any other pair of eyes, she was, once more, properly indifferent; so long as she was Venus to him she could be Plain Jane to every other man. Done right, love is private, a compelling but cryptic script. "Lie down with me," she beckoned, unclasping his belt, scrabbling at his zipper.

And then they made love with the ardor of teenagers; bare-chested, they went to ground. Pushing him beneath her, she gave him her tensed nipples while her hand, slipping below his waistband, sought command of his broad phallus. Desire swept over them in waves, a long-awaited storm. Their kissing traced a terse, hurried evolution: first, a few bashful lip-holds; next, a flurry of flitting tongue-thrusts; finally, a full, open-mouthed communion. After this they digressed, nibbling and licking in out-of-the-way places; a fury possessed them to taste every surface, reclaim every domain.

"Oh!" she moaned, rolling off when she could endure no more. "Oh, Adam, undress me!"

Sitting up, he clutched the sides of her one-piece and peeled it away, admiring the result. In this morning room, which the sun entered obliquely, casting blurry rhomboids through the dusty window panes, the sight of her lying so unrepentantly nude on the slate-colored rug seemed almost compositional, studio art. "Magnificent," he appraised.

"Yours for the taking," she purred.

Pivoting onto his knees, he dropped his pants, freed his loins. He liked it almost better than sex itself, this pause before the act. There was no room in it for anything other than raw anticipation, unconstrained glee. "Lucky me," he said.

Wordlessly, she moved to prime him, letting her mouth go slack. Out of practice with fellatio, she felt tentative, unskilled. His cock seemed a curious and unwieldy thing; she had nearly forgotten the dank, obscure taste of it, its palpable ridges and veins. The staccato pressure of his spongy tip reached deeper than she remembered; she wondered if chastity had enlarged him.

"No, stop—stop!" Adam pleaded, pulling out. He was at the edge, his testicles brimming with an intolerable sweetness. "Your turn."

Helplessly, she unhanded him and lay back, prepared to give up the last part of herself which had been held in reserve. Soon she felt the warmth of his tongue on her pelt, felt him part the delicate petals beneath, home in. She had always been able to come this way; she was in the fortunate minority. Yet if she had a preference, it was for orthodoxy, coitus Mennonite-style. "Come up," she said as his tempo was increasing. "Fuck me."

"If you insist."

"I do."

Presently he obliged her. And, at last, the Falks were a couple again, a jubilant and flourishing unity.

Until late that afternoon, they made love almost hourly. And if their performance in the first session had been competent, an average erotic sequence, they improved upon it successively in the rest. They choreographed, they improvised. They tested precarious angles and offbeat rhythms. Props were introduced, sound effects explored. Their best moments were postponed, then prolonged. But at last they grew exhausted; overused, their genitals went numb. It came time for discussion and review.

"I must have stored it all up," Marion sighed contentedly. Haphazardly draped in a displaced sheet, she lay sprawled against Adam's side. For the follow-on shenanigans they had retreated to the bedroom.

"Stored what up?"

Backhandedly, she stroked his stubbled cheek. The urge to touch him, to confirm his nearness, had become continuous. "Oh, all that cheesy advice you get in the check-out aisle: 'Ten Tips on How to Be More Satisfied,' 'Do's and Don'ts in the Sack'—you've seen the captions."

"You mean you actually read that stuff?"

"Once in a while, if I'm in a slow line. Everybody does." She gloated, "And do you know what? They're right about a couple of things."

As he listened to it, her voice seemed to come from a place that was not outside him. It was the same perception he had had during their courtship: they had seemed immersed in each other, consubstantial. "I'll get us a subscription," he promised.

Unashamedly, Marion touched her own breast; in the afterglow of so many arousals her areolas still tingled. "Our bodies are complex," she posited. "They ought to come with manuals. Those magazines are the next best thing."

"Marriage is complex."

A fitful breeze had begun to rattle the sashes; on the waters around them, yachtsmen would be taking in sail. Anticipating a chill, she pulled more covers over herself and nestled against the lax warm flesh below his shoulder. "We're finally getting the knack of it," she averred.

With a spiraling finger he wound a strand of her hair onto his forefinger, while against the tawny ceiling he foresaw their future: they would succeed, finally, at filling in the subtlest and most precious shades of companionship; their happiness would be topped with mundanities; together they would shop for groceries, plan menus, tend a vegetable garden. "What took us so long?" he asked.

"We were young," Marion consoled. "We were incomplete." Turning over, she clutched him possessively across the ribcage, underscoring that she was speaking of the past. "We needed to fend each other off a little as we matured."

He passed his vacant arm reciprocally over hers, establishing a full overlap. His appetite for his wife had become limitless; his soul could not achieve enough points of contact with her to feel sated. "We shouldn't blame ourselves," he said. "Most people fumble through life; we've been no exception."

"We've been thoroughly average, haven't we?"

"Quite."

In the past five days they had propounded the bulk of a necessary catechism, an expiating recitation of acknowledgments and avowals. There was no need for more of this just now. For the rest, they could proceed at an easier pace.

"How about an activity?" Marion chirped.

"Do you have something in mind?"

"I found a kite in the attic, strung and all."

"This is the perfect place for one," he agreed, quickly cottoning to the idea.

"We can take it over to the east end."

"Yes, by the bluffs."

"Bet I can get dressed before you do!"

Outside, they encountered a day very different from the one they had left: frothing seas, twenty knots of wind. To the west, dark clouds were bunching, packing force. In an hour they might see squalls. Adam had always cherished the advent of a cold front; its intensity, its *Sturm und Drang*, inspired him to call up a braver, more impetuous version of himself.

"When was the last time we did this?" Marion shouted into a gust. Whipped by the impertinent air, her eyes were freely tearing.

Though she was trying to prompt a recollection of their last sortie for this purpose with Sarah and David, his mind skipped a generation further back, retrieving an anguishing scene. He pictured an autumn hillside on a cold, clear day, his father next to him, coaching. Then this insert, with partial audio: His brother, Peter, had been there also, and it had been his brother, his rival, who had handled the kite first, deftly maneuvering it through a series of loops and stalls, crossing and recrossing invisible rips aloft. "Remember to take in the line if it starts to dip," his father had warned when it was his turn, but to no avail. Under his command the craft had plummeted to the earth, snapping a strut. His brother had worn a smirk for hours afterwards. "It's been a while," he dissimulated.

A three-minute walk brought them to the launch point, a treeless knoll just in from the headland. Dropping to their knees, they set about assembling the air-frame; unfurled, the kite took on the appearance of a craft with swept-back wings, a fighter or tubby missile.

"Looks like a high-performance model," Adam judged when they were done. "Let's see how she flies."

He released, and she spooled. In the robust breeze their charge ascended decisively, seeming to yearn for altitude. As twine was fed out they watched its red and blue panel's transition into ambiguity, the neutral color of all high-flying objects. Gradually it seemed to grow almost independent of them, to become a free-willed creation.

"You're doing a fine job with it!" he called. *And fine you are, too,* he thought. Had he been camera-prone, this would have been a must-have shot: his wife, his partner and soul-mate, the interpreter of his spunk, not as young as once, but still comely, still fair, captured on this stark, dramatic terrain, in such a determined and hopeful pose. Framed against the bare rock and the tossing sea, her gaze uplifted towards the unquiet sky, she again seemed ready to believe—not just in them, but in some broader proposition, the purposefulness of our human lives.

"It almost flies itself!" she exclaimed, praising the design. "You try it!"

Obligingly, he took the spindle. Side-by-side they watched the tiny chevron struggle for greater heights. And it was then that they noticed it: nearly straight above them, a duplicate radiance, a supernumerary aura, pressing through the clouds. It was as if the five o'clock sun had reverted to its midday position. Was it simply a refraction? A band of errant rays bending back through the atmosphere? Perhaps. But assuredly it was a light too bright to derive from the plenary moon, or one of the larger planets, or any other reckonable source.

There was an otherness about Clarence; along some elusive but providential dimension, he measured out as extraordinary or uncanny. They both perceived it, but just barely so; it was a quality which gadded across the limits of their senses, a feature they discerned falteringly, a phenomenon observed as if through clouds of fog.

From the cocktail hour that evening, they could have given this example:

They were in the living room, halfway through the first round, chatting up current events—the coming elections, the latest flicks—when Clarence appeared to pass hors d'oeuvres. The same species of talk continued to spill from their lips, but in his presence it suddenly tasted of prattle. Subliminally, they perceived that the details of the world they lived in did not concern this man; unaccountably, they understood that he was from a different era. The refulgence, the gaiety in his eyes confirmed it. Clarence was with them, but he was not. He was in time, but he was not. He had one foot in the untold aspect of things.

In the life of every couple there are certain dinners, certain evenings, that achieve a special resonance; they gather and magnify our affections; they render us weightless. For the Falks, the paradigm of all such occasions, one they would have cherished regardless of a divorce, was their night in the Oak Room. Let us invoke the scene, inhabit the mood:

It was late March, that time of year in New York which spawns an anticipation of winter's end: a hint of warmth collecting in the side streets, buds forming on the early shrubs. Their engagement was so new that it still seemed rough copy. They were at that stage of betrothal, intensified by their youth, where the sense of good fortune mixes with disbelief, where one simultaneously feels rescued from uncertainty and deprived of further choice. To pass beyond this they needed to enlist each other not just as lovers but as colluders, partners in some grand and unifying impropriety. And as it is with all the best pranks, the giddiest larks, this one was impromptu.

They had intended, that day, to come in from Connecticut and see a show, an Off-Broadway revival of, *A Month in the Country,* then return to his parents', where they had been staying during his spring break. By intermission, however, the currents of passion had overtaken them; the thought of going back to de facto chaperones and separate bedrooms became insupportable. "Let's get a room," she had pleaded as they sipped chardonnay on the mezzanine. Unable to refuse her—when does any red-blooded male refuse such a request?—and unable to countenance economies, brook half-measures, he had led across town forthwith, escorting her proudly into the Algonquin, signing them in as "Mr. and Mrs." A single credit card swipe had ticketed them past the palace guards: the supercilious desk clerks, officious bellhops, and bull-necked house detectives. Ah, the virtues of plastic! Yet the three-part sexual escapade that ensued was only a prelude, a set of horizontal aerobics that served to burn off their lust and kindle their appetites; when they dressed and came downstairs again they were ready to explore another level of indulgence, what it is that surpasses an orgasm.

What he remembers most is the strawberries bathed in melted, dark chocolate.

For her it is the 1964 Chateau Rothchild.

Rapt they were on either account, transported by their senses to a place where time eddies and diffuses away from itself, leaving just the fullness, the sumptuousness of the moment.

She recalls an infiltration of warmth, and briefly, reaching the conviction that the common objects around them had become luminous, softly tinged with amber light.

He recalls a perception that his metabolism was accelerating, that the atoms within his body had mustered themselves into a dance, a sort of biochemical hora.

They both recall the phenomenology of merger, the keen and distinct awareness that their souls were bleeding into each other, combining.

And that is when they were joined: not fifteen months later in a traditional church service, but there, then, immured by those stately panels, attended by men in evening dress.

After that, to be sure, there were many other excellent repasts. From Loch-Ober to Nob Hill they would set foot in dozens of tony eateries, a bevy of three-stars. But some standards prove insuperable, and in all those subsequent adventures in fine dining they had failed to recapture the signal enchantment of that night in the Oak Room— failed that is, until now.

It wasn't the baked ham. Or the glazed carrots, or the romaine salad. Their dinner, as had been the case each night, was competently prepared, but there was nothing extraordinary about it, no remarkable savoriness. Rather, it was what the meal seemed to carry with it—the next level of understanding, a heightened experience of at-oneness— that abides.

It spilled over them in a palpable wash, like the warmth of the day through parting clouds.

"I like the way you've done your hair tonight," he was saying, admiring the swept-back curves at her temples. "You've opened it up, somehow."

Gazing away, Marion panned the gray rim of the ocean, the rugged now-familiar sequence of islands leading out to the horizon. "That's what being up here has done for us," she submitted.

"More on that, please."

"It's opened us up; it's given us access to each other." Turning back to him, she extended her hand across the table, offering a mea culpa, an apology. "I was so closed off to you, Adam. I'm sorry."

By the persistent daylight he considered his wife exactly and scientifically: just as she was. He saw the slightly nervous pucker of her lower lip; he saw the splotchy, unattended blemish on her chin; he saw the skin below her eyes aging to a parchment thickness. He saw her all in all. And what he beheld was lovely. "We were a pair of facades," he told her. "We were protecting ourselves."

Still clear-eyed, she clenched his hand until their bones seemed to touch. "From this day forward," she vouched, "you shall have my whole heart."

"And you, mine," he returned, mirroring her consecratory tone.

Then, because silence was better and more expressive, they offered no more words. A segment of their lives, like a section in a book, had been entirely revised; all the ungainly prose, the narrative stumps, had been extirpated. The process, though, had been tiring; they had earned a rest, a pause, a caesura.

For Adam it was an opportunity to obtain passage on a trade ship, to imagine himself piloting a barque around the local shoals, out onto parlous seas.

For Marion it was a chance to study the ribbed texture, the graded hues, of the Bay; to trace the feathery brushstrokes a painter would employ to transfer the scene onto canvas.

For both of them it was a time to drink a full draught of the detail, the deliciousness that is the world.

And when they came out of it they brought with them a new insight.

"It's more than you said," Adam intoned.

"What, dear?"

"It's not just that we've found access to each other—we've also opened up to ourselves, to our better natures. I feel like I can draw from the best parts of myself again."

Marion peered out into the blue dusk, the immaculate twilight. Within the atmosphere—more proximate, it seemed, than on the previous night—she detected a flawless presence, some motive and healing authority. This could not be just chance, she knew; their reconciliation, indisputably, had been granted. "It's true," she agreed. "We're all of what we were—more, even."

Noticing her preoccupation, he turned to find the source, gazing where she gazed, and now, at last, he saw it, too: a vague superfluity, an infinitesimal sparkle—something. And that was the point at which the Falks, together, began to cross over into a new philosophy. Until then they had been rationalists, of the belief that we are bound to a reality of hard rules and knowable causes; but on that evening they became wonderers and stargazers, inclined to treasure the cosmos most for the secrets it withholds, devotees of its mysteries.

In the courthouses of central New Jersey the clerks and stenographers—the judges, too—are still talking about it, and from the white glove firms down to the lowliest hacks there's a sense of impending privation, the concern that, in the future, there may be fewer honey pots left out on the table, less easy money. The majority of these brothers and sisters before the Bar, suffice it to say, feel blindsided, betrayed; and if there is a smaller number who do not rue the chastening they have received—well, they're on salary, of course, or work strictly by the hour.

The whole stir is so much more surprising allowing for its source. Abrasive and shamelessly self-promoting (viz.: the perennial ads on the back of the yellow pages), a rottweiler in the courtroom, ambulance chaser par excellence, Peter Falk was, until now, an archangel among the demons, one of the local barons of personal injury. Hence it was both a spectacle and shock for all concerned to see him on the Friday night news renouncing his bread and butter and sounding a battle cry for, yes, tort reform.

"The system is grotesque," he is quoted as saying. "Mammoth judgments are levied against defendants who are not logically at fault. Greed has trumped justice; self-interest has blotted out common sense."

The initial, cynical response was that he was just grandstanding, blustering his way, perhaps, towards a political launch. For Peter has long had a reputation as a chess master; his moves are always plotted to produce either tactical result or strategic advantage. But on this occasion the naysayers are getting their comeuppance. In the weeks and months since his declamation, attorney Falk has proven to be nothing less than a changed man, Saul of Tarsus. He has winnowed his practice; he no longer pursues consumer product litigation or accident claims. His focus has turned towards social causes, the environment. The Nature Conservatory is now a client, as is the A.C.L.U. And now he works on the clock, or, increasingly, pro bono.

Recently, the newspapers have revisited Peter's case. His has become something of a human-interest story, a psychological conundrum. How is it, the question is asked, that a man so accomplished at such a lucrative, albeit ethically permeable trade suddenly finds the inspiration, the will, to step aside? Was it simply a build-up of guilt? Did his conscience rebel? Or was there a health concern? A family problem? Tell us, they have pleaded. Give us the scoop.

To date, however, his answers have not satisfied; the familiar themes have not obtained. He denies receiving an ultimatum from his cardiologist. There is no mid-life crisis. He is not gearing for retirement. His turnabout, he insists, is an enigma even to him. He knows only that it came to him suddenly, almost as a revelation, that he was on the wrong path. His brother, he tells, is a physician in Massachusetts. He would like to be more like him. He would like to be caring and kind. He would like to give back. So now he is trying.

His eyes, to her, appeared unexpectedly variegated, bearing within their olive green irises an array of minute flaxen spindles, a subtle counterstain; hers, to him, were clearer and even more cerulean, the color of our aspirations, than he had allowed himself to remember. They had not been able to study each other like this—close-up, continuously—since the days of their courtship, since infatuation had ceded to proprietorship, passion to convenience.

"Perhaps the island isn't taken next week," he whispered. "I could cancel a few patients; we could stay on." Naked, haloed by the auburn light of a single antique lamp, they lay facing each other in bed; across the down quilt cocooning them their four hands nuzzled and intertwined. Upright and properly attired, they would have resembled a couple at the end of a dance, or the beginning of a proposal.

"Not on your life!" she protested, jostling him with her toes. "I just want to get you home." Concurrently, a frank, almost tawdry, love-struck expression spread across her face, and briefly, he was bound by its spell. He had not known her to be capable of such mooning, such an unreserved display of affection. Even during the best times, she had signaled her affiliation for him through a repertoire of endearing yet restrained gestures: a palm to his chest, a finger slipped through his belt loop.

"But we can't go there again," he told her, picking up the metaphor. Marion cocked her head in perplexity.

"Look at what's happening to us up here," he explained. "We've extricated ourselves from stasis. We're entering new territory. It's what happy couples do. They're restless, inquisitive. They journey through life. Existentially, they don't stay in one place."

She raised herself up onto one elbow to digest this admonition. His words, she conceived, were ushering her around a psychological corner, easing her towards a parallax view of herself. He was right, of course: complacency was unhealthy; she was capable of more. Her spirit could not thrive without having free range. She said, "You are wise, my husband."

"Pshaw."

Dreamily, she peered out through a misted window, into the indigo darkness, toward the life to come. "You'll be with me along the way?" she asked.

"I will."

Rugs she decided; she had been flirting with the notion for some time. Her friend, Gabriella, a lean, intense, childless woman of Spanish and Armenian descent was considering expanding her business, a high-end shop in Weymouth; she had asked Marion to come on as an assistant, offered to teach her the trade. There seemed much to like about the proposition—it would provide *raison d'être*, an excuse to travel, and entrée into some of the grander homes on the South Shore; it might even induce her to learn something about the Middle East— and little to dislike: she would have flexible hours, no partnership risk. A year from now, she could imagine herself dickering with wholesalers on the lower East Side; two or three could find her on the streets of Tabriz. "I might try to do something in retail," she allowed.

Level with them, Adam admired the symmetry of her ample, high-slung breasts, even as gravity skewed them to the side. Hers was the torso of a chorus girl. "Anything in particular?"

"Gabriella is thinking of opening up another storefront. She's asked me to help out."

Effortlessly, as if she had just been their dinner guest, Adam pulled up a detailed image. Dark-complexioned, exotic, and though well into her thirties, still curiously unattached, Gabriella had long been on that roster of women he would have considered as prospects after a divorce. Years ago, on a whim, while scouting out Christmas presents, he had slipped into her boutique. Had it been wishful thinking, or had she come on to him up in the musty loft where she displayed the throw rugs? It was decidedly a moot point, for he had gladly reentered that state of commitment, and the corresponding libidinal disposition, where other women, even the most alluring ones, were nothing more than *objets d'art,* graceful ornaments. Blamelessly, Marion's was the only flesh he craved; once again his appetites were wholly monogamous. "I think that's a great idea," he said earnestly. "You've always had a decorative eye."

"It would mean"—solicitously, she stroked his forehead, as if to counter any worry developing behind it—"it would mean I wouldn't be around as much."

"To darn my stockings, you mean? I'll manage. To love is to not limit."

Wistfully, with a slow, doting finger, she mussed the hair at his temples, turning out a few gray interlopers. This was not just the mature expression of the man she had married, she realized: this person exceeded that. "You'll give up your stay-at-home wife?"

"Everyone's life should be novelistic, dearest. There would be no richness if there were only one motif."

"But I won't lose track of the main theme," she promised.

"Ah. And how would you describe that?"

"Devotion." She pronounced the word evenly and summarily, easing back down beside him. "Belonging to you as fully as I can."

It was a statement neither one of them dared to crowd; respectfully, they let it stand by itself, moating it in a protective silence. Outside, the night had become crepitant; its very molecularity seemed astir. It was palpable to them now: the growth at the cusp, the greening. The body of their marriage had been buttressed and rehabilitated; out of the stalk new shoots were forming. Ahead of them lay the work of a new season.

"That's all I could ask," he murmured, slipping his fingers along her pillow and under her cheek until her head, her admiring countenance, appeared to be held in his hand. "And if I go off in some new direction myself, you shall have the same."

Marion languidly blinked, holding her eyes shut for a replenishing extra beat. To assimilate even pleasant news she often required an interval to settle herself. "What were you thinking of?" she asked.

He unveiled, succinctly, the yield from myriad rounds of soul-searching, his projections for a viable second career: "There are a couple of options. I could work in public policy, or teach science, perhaps."

Her lips, hovering perpendicularly above his palm, curled into a parenthesis; she was pleased. "I think you should get a job at the Department of Health. It could lead to other things."

In her gaze he saw pride, optimism, and a balmy knowingness— the look of a longsuffering parent whose child has finally come to value their advice.

"Deep down, Adam," she continued, "you're a politician. You love to shmooze."

Pegged, as usual. Inexorably, he had grown to regret—no, to loathe—the insularity, the priestly confidentiality, entailed in his profession. After all the years assuaging private gripes and unmentionable ailments, he had reached the tipping point. He was ready to abandon the confessional, shed the frock. Yet to do so, he realized, had waited upon this: her dependable presence, her encouragement. Love enables; love empowers. "You're right," he said, squaring himself to the prospect of real change. "I've taken care of people long enough. There has to be something else out there for me."

"Turn out the light," she said, nosing the patch of skin behind his ear. "Maybe we can find it in the dark."

Throughout the night, an element in all their dreams, there was movement. Not the steady, lulling motion of travel, nor the rhythmic pattern of some engineered action, but a persistent, though uneven, concatenation of slow turnings and sluings, archings and easings. At first they might have judged the disquiet to be simple restiveness, their found happiness rippling over onto the fringes of sleep, but as it continued—and even increased—they must have guessed it to be purposive, the signature of some restorative process, for they let it play out; trustingly they remained submerged, willfully hunkering below the plane of consciousness. Yet though their fancies incorporated and interpreted the same kinetics, they were constituted in different media.

When Marion moved, it was through air. Whether her body spun or twisted or merely tensed, it did so within a fragrant atmosphere, cooled by a lambent flow. In an early scene she was a swift, or a martin, a nimble little bird swooping, swerving, sashaying over purple-tinted fields at sunset; in a later one she was a figure skater scudding across a frozen pond, perfecting axels and pirouettes on virgin ice.

Adam's exploits, by contrast, were aqueous. Initially he was a trout; tail-finning over a gravel bed in a Western stream, he felt the spring runoff burble past his smooth integument. Subsequently he became an otter; deep within a foam-topped pool he wriggled and cork-screwed his way around sunken limbs and branches, hunting up minnows, rooting for crayfish.

They soloed in their dreams at the outset; there was little sense of the company or propinquity of other beings, coincident life. By what seemed the middle of the night, however, they began to discern vague presences, illusory forms. Then began a succession of evanescent contacts, skin of a like texture intersecting with theirs, glancing across their hips, torsos, and thighs. At first they conceived themselves to be in the midst of a multitude—a flock of swallows chasing an insect swarm, a school of silverfish streaming with the current—but by degrees, the number of entities pressing against them coalesced into only one.

In Marion's imagination there appeared a dance partner. On a balmy night, under a spangled sky, on the deck of a great ship, they were light-footing through a waltz, or a tango. Though she could not make out his face, there was much about the man—the pliancy of his muscles, the low contours of his physique—that was familiar and accommodating. He, also, seemed to know her, to anticipate her mechanics, her body's sway and range, as if they had long practiced together. Who could he be, she puzzled, this gent, this charmer, who cornered and revolved with her in perfect sync? She believed he must be a distillation of many men, her conception of the ideal.

And Adam, too, still waterborne, now a merman, was joined by a counterpart. Ebulliently, yet in silence, her lithe form cavorted with him in an iridescent sea. Skin-to-skin above and scale-to-scale below, they rolled and twisted around each other in a lazy, spiraling dalliance, an anonymous marine minuet.

Doubtlessly they will not retain as much detail as this in their memories of that night—even less of the sequencing, the evolution of its images—though some will set. For it is of the nature of dreams to soothe our cares and reinvigorate our souls and then withdraw, like a watchful mother who steals into our room to set the sheets back over us. Yet what they will most certainly recall, having since traded many descriptions of it, is their awakening: how their other senses, reviving, combined to reveal what touch alone could not.

Marion, first, saw eyes that were avocado green, heard murmurings in a resonant baritone.

Adam woke to the buttery taste of half-parted lips, the pheromonal scents of expectant flesh.

Then they both continued with what, in their dreams, they had already commenced: an additional bout of robust and inventive lovemaking.

SATURDAY

"Good morning, my owl."

Posing before the bathroom mirror, passingly *soi-distant*, Adam observed himself grin at the rebirth of this discarded moniker. In their formative days she had applied it derivatively to him after he had begun to call her "cat," and then, inevitably, "pussycat." The name had always resonated pleasingly with his conceit that a judicious bent, a precocious sagacity, had accompanied the questioning and philosophical mindset he seemed to have inherited from his father. "And good morning to you, you purr-fect creature," he crooned, looping his arm around the middle part of her, his hand coming to rest in the pliant recess above her hip. Affectingly, she had requested his presence as she completed her morning ablutions.

"Well, here we are before we've arranged ourselves," she declared, peering at their reflection. "It's the raw us."

Deliberatively, he assessed, "On the whole, I don't think we're doing so badly, for early middle age."

It was a corollary of their refurbished bond, their newly reaffirmed commitedness, that they should begin to anticipate the first nips of aging, the petulant joints and faltering glands, the brittler sinews and filmier vision that lay ahead. Disclosure and discussion of their physical woes was a comfort they had provided less and less to each other during their period of estrangement, even as the number and frequency of these had increased. She had not heard that he was considering a carpal tunnel release; he was unaware that she had recently had an abnormal pap. Now they were free to admit their symptoms, expound their anxieties. Leaning forward to pluck a stray lash, she asked, "How's your back?"

He gave her a concise, laudatory squeeze. "All the horizontal calisthenics we've been doing have loosened it up, thank you very much. I'll be canceling my chiropractor's appointments."

"Good," she said, setting her tweezers down, her work of depilation done. "I need you in good working order; I need you——"

He heard her tone shift, drop into the sober, measured range she had once used with the children to get them to heed some principal of fairness, or desist from raucous play—"I need you to be well."

"But I am, sweetie. Just a few cricks in the machine; that's all."

Marion sighed, unable to squelch a burst of morbid thinking, resurgent fatalism, and her gaze scoured the glass as if searching for something she hoped might be embedded within it: an encryption, a shibboleth. "I don't mean just that," she said, clasping the hand that held her. "I want you—us—to have longevity; I want us to grow old together."

In their early forties, they were still young enough to take it as unfathomable, a perversion of the natural order, whenever someone their age was stricken. Lymphoma, heart disease, colon cancer: already these scourges had started to winnow their Christmas card list. Just last winter, Fred Erlich, a sailing acquaintance, a great wooly mastodon of a man, had collapsed at a business lunch, expiring face-down in a plate of pasta; a few months before that one of Marion's Sarah Lawrence hallmates had succumbed to a rare parasitic infection acquired while on sabbatical in Mexico. To the best of their knowledge, each had previously been in good health. *How precarious our lives all are*, Adam thought. *We balance atop the eroded rim, the cresting wave; we rise up out of the earth for only so long, and then return to it, to duff and dust.* "I'll do my best," he promised: "More vegetables, less animal fat. My gender is against me, though; the man usually goes first."

Marion had yet to achieve a firm conceptualization of the hereafter—its presumptive accessibility, its shape and extension, its moral relevance. Most often she thought of it pantheistically, in the guise of a kind of blithe and final diffuseness; one was subsumed into the materiality, the subatomic framework, of all living things; one's perpetuity spanned endless revolutions of the Krebs cycle. As to whether there might be colloquy, a degree of interchange among the departed, she had also been agnostic. But now that it appeared that it would be death, indeed, that would part them, the prospect of nullity, the possibility that we abut an utter cold blankness, loomed disagreeably. Earnestly, she told him, "It doesn't seem fair."

"What, women getting a few more years? I've always though it was your recompense for the agonies of childbirth."

"No, that we can't know what the end is like, or if it really is the end. It's not the dying that bothers me, it's the uncertainty that comes with it."

He sensed her mind struggling, grappling with angst. For as long as he had known her she had loathed delving into issues that were unresolvable. Tenderly, he proposed, "There *is* a way we can face it together."

In the mirror, her eyes searched for his. "How?"

"We can agree to be commingled." In its aftermath the phrase sounded impersonal, legalistic. "We can have our ashes mixed," he amended. "In death we can merge."

She considered his suggestion concretely, even sensually, picturing their incinerated remains blended and stirred. If sex was an apposition, a conjunction, a joyous pollination, then this might be something more. Breathing in, she sought to imagine it by inhaling—ingesting—his musky effluvium, the emissions of his suet. At best she did so remotely; even here, in these close confines, the essence of him seemed to slip by. To intercept her husband fully, to meet his every rank particle, toss with the elements that composed him: that would be unity. "I'm surprised," she confessed. "I thought you wanted traditional arrangements."

He scoffed. "What, a pine box? If there's a resurrection, I don't want to come back as gristle and bones. Cremation is certainly tidier." Hesitating, he admitted a possible hitch. "In your case, though, there might be objections." He was referring to her ancestral resting place, a rose-marble mausoleum ringed by a score of plots on the outskirts of Evanston. Interred below the floor of the tomb, her great-great-grandfather, it was rumored, lay wrapped in gilded cerements, an American pharaoh. "Aren't they reserving a space, or a drawer, for you?"

"It's becoming optional, in my generation. The kids won't be disinherited if I go elsewhere."

Within a marriage, there are many pacts. Some are fixed at the outset; others are devised en route. At their stage, they should not have expected to discover a domain entirely free of negotiated expectations, yet here it was. In broaching it they felt delinquent and irreverent, as though the observance of proper etiquette would have called for an agreement on this matter long before.

"So you would be available," he asked sheepishly, "to join me?"

With no trace of ambivalence, she passed her hand under his night shirt, pressing it to his spine. "I am," she said.

Then, tacitly, with an embrace witnessed only by their reflections, they sealed it: a pledge to be immolated and combined, a promise never to part.

They do not recall it now, any more than they can recall any other component of their time with him—all of that has been lost, necessarily expunged from that fickle reservoir in the mind from which we retrieve, like keepsakes, the signal and the trivial, the collectibles and the etceteras of our experience—but it was during that morning's breakfast that Clarence began to step away from them, sidling gently into a mystery, an airy and preconceived oblivion.

Imagine a flickering image, or a weakening signal: his presence became staccato; sometimes it was perceptible to them, sometimes not. Or conceive of him as a figure stitching in and out of time, skirting an invisible threshold, a border between this world and some other. When he was with them he continued to attend to his duties, but when he was not they found themselves doing what was needed, picking up the slack. They collaborated, if you will, with a figment; they partnered with an illusion.

They remember none of this today, to be sure. As they look back on that day and that week, there is no recollection of a third party, a curmudgeonly personal assistant. And if they possess any cognizance of special circumstances or extraordinary phenomena that prevailed during that interval it consists mostly in this: that the stock of bread that they had on hand did not diminish; indeed, that it appeared to have increased.

Had the question been directly put to him, the young David Falk would never have disputed the importance of honest self-appraisal, of achieving a full and accurate knowledge of one's talents, eccentricities, and shortcomings. An observing ego, they called it. Right mind. Terms culled from freshman psychology. In his conception, however, the knack of effective self-examination was acquired gradually, through a process spanning many years. And at the age of twenty, the bulk of this apprenticeship, he had assumed lay well ahead of him; it was to be taken up after graduation, played out on the chancy terrain beyond the palace walls.

Looking back on that attitude does not cause David chagrin; he does not blame himself for having held commonplace notions of growing up, finding a path. Defaulting to the majority view, the median event is as natural as it is cautious. How many of us, after all, have it all shown to them in an instant? How routine are epiphanies? No, Captain Falk does not upbraid himself for the fact that he was once directionless and undisciplined; he simply gives thanks for a visit paid to him by the Fates on a muggy morning in June long ago.

To this day he remembers the scene vividly: the brackish stillness, the monotone sky, the sluggish coastline. He had had his parents' house to himself, and as usual, abused the privilege. Uncollected, the detritus of several days' revelry was beginning to obstruct hallways and obfuscate countertops. Beer cans massed in corners; cigarette butts speckled the carpets. Within David's circle of friends these bacchanalian landscapes were becoming the stuff of legend: far from fastidious themselves, none of them dared host such ventures into utter dissoluteness, such faithful renditions of Kerouac and Burroughs. Yet of these excursions into profligacy he would say even now that they bore the mark of a leader: regardless of the endeavor, you are the first, or the only one, to go beyond the point where others balk.

When he tries to comprehend the change that transpired that day in ordinary terms, and not as a matter of celestial influence, he turns to the maxim from Blake: "The road of excess leads to the palace of wisdom." It could be that his about-face was the proof of it; it could be that there is only so much of the reprobate, a limited capacity for self-indulgence, in each one of us. When it is spent we lose the option of purblindness; we must see ourselves clearly. But what he cannot reckon is its abruptness, how swiftly it came over him. Barely awake, his faculties still at loose ends, he recalls a sudden, overpowering nausea as intense as if he had been placed in forced proximity with something putrid and decomposing; that coupled with the sense of being confined to a hall of mirrors, of being bombarded by his own blowzy and feckless image. It was within minutes, it seemed, that he grasped the magnitude of his irresponsibility and rejected it. The chrysalis opened. Reform was initiated. A useful and decent person was born.

Those that know David now—his wife and children, his fellow officers, the enlisted men who serve under him—would be hard-pressed to derive the boy from the man. Although few would call him a martinet, neither do they underestimate his belief in regimentation, the importance of keeping all sails trimmed. Approaching fifty, he still runs marathons; his drinking is limited to a glass of bubbly on ceremonial occasions; and, if he possesses any vice, it is certainly his obsessive chess-playing. The knock on him is that he can be a little dull, but, in truth, he doesn't mind. Better that than to be perceived as rough-edged or immoderate. For war is a serious business, and he is one of its top executives. At present he commands a missile-class destroyer, the U.S.S. *Webster*. No doubt, however, he will soon make admiral. He will become one of the archons. He will move on to higher things.

Adam had never had the kind of mind that can lift complex sensations, retainable impressions, from descriptive narrative; his right brain had never embraced the appeal of "travel writing," and, hence, on those odd occasions, such as this, when a stray *National*

Geographic, or its ilk, found its way into his hands, he became a page-flipper, absorbing only the photo content, impassively glimpsing wide-angled shots of African savannas, slice-of-life scenes from Old Europe. The issue in his hands, *Leisure Pursuits,* was, to boot, pure ersatz, surely a gratuitous publication, half ads. Its montages were grainy, its layout unkempt. Unable to home in on any of the text, his gaze slipped and slithered through the folios, veering off not infrequently onto the terra firma of actuality, what there was to observe of the world close by.

He could not help noticing, for instance, the very composition of the air, the presence, within it, of multitudinous particles. The oblique morning sun, fanning into the living room as an array of lemony diagonals, highlighted a floating arabesque, a miasma of minute squiggles and specks. Further afield, his eye caught on the wear-and-tear in the upholstery: here a sprung cushion, there a fraying ruff. In his distractedness, in fact, he seemed to perceive more about the space, a more intimate level of detail, than had this been his conscious purpose. Voilà: "lateral awareness."

Towards the back of the magazine he reapplied himself, making a concerted attempt to peruse a feature on San Antonio. Conditional on his finding a suitable junket, he thought, the city—which he had never seen—might someday warrant a short visit. Gamely, he settled into a few paragraphs touting romantic walks along the river front, a day trip to see the old missions, but despite his best effort, the notion of going anywhere in Texas remained unappealing. He deplored the cowboy mentality, all swagger and braggadocio; bronco bars and mariachi bands did not appeal. No, a city had to have gravitas, a respectable aesthetic, for him to allocate time to it. Galveston did not stack against Seville or Valencia.

The magazine thus lost its hold on him again and, this time, as if freed from imperceptible moorings, his eyes floated upwards, rising over the top of those insipid pages to perceive something far more prepossessing: his wife's visage, softened by a mood of pure contentment, perfect complacency, as it studied him, holding an assured smile…

"Dearest," he intoned, looking west across the passage to Rockport, "you've read Virginia Woolf, haven't you?" Though the weather was iffy—a wall of sooty, muscular clouds was building up over the mainland—they had chosen to have lunch once again in what had become their favorite venue, a pair of low-profile chairs set on a grassy patch just in from the southern tip of the island.

Hunched forward, on the verge of opening up their picnic basket, Marion had paused to admire the intricate floral design sewn on its lid. "Naturally." She quipped, "She's required reading for all of us Sisters of Lilith. Half of one of my courses at Sarah Lawrence was devoted to her."

Adam's voice narrowed to a rhetorical, academic strain. "In *To the Lighthouse*, then, how do you interpret the water imagery?" Though, when he read fiction, it was generally current fare, to create overlap with his wife he had occasionally suffered through one of the Victorian or early Modernist titles. Against his better judgment, one or two had even appealed.

Marion sat back, not so much to consider the question as to savor the fact that it had been asked. Albeit sophomoric at times, they had once sustained an intellectual resonance; agreeably, they had served as each other's foils. "I think it's multi-determined," she replied, picturing the Ramsays at dusk perambulating—was it?—the Cornish coast. "The water is baptismal, of course; for Woolf it represents the transformational power of art, the gap we close by participating in the aesthetic process, between plurality and unity, between subjectivity and truth. It also stands for the female principle, the passive-receptive mode, which is at the root of all creativity." *Not bad*, she wanted to say, after twenty years' absence from the carrels. A reprise of the phase when teachers had encouraged her to be polemical and expansive, to luxuriate in the elaborateness of thought.

Uncertain of his purpose in starting this discussion, Adam perceived it now: he sought additional proof of their rapprochement. If they could discourse even-handedly, without tipping into invidiousness, then their amity was sound. Stretching his arm toward the Bay, which had taken on a peridot hue under the darkening skies, he countered, "One could say that the water represents Death, and that the characters' journey to the lighthouse symbolizes our struggle to conquer it."

"Ah!" She let this little exclamation stand alone for a moment, and her features tightened into a quizzical configuration. Heuristically, she was engaged. "You're right; there's that level, too. That's what I like about Woolf. Her writing is so impressionistic; it supports a wide range of themes."

"Yes."

They should set it aside, they knew: this little rounded cycle of discussion, harmoniously concluded. Concise as it was, it constituted a sufficient illustration, an adequate reminder, that the words, the terms of art, were still there, as was the knack of critique. Their future would see these skills plied. There would be gallery openings and Ibsen productions; there would be violin concertos and handicraft shows; there would be no dearth of opportunities to trade opinions, speak about culture. But for now it was enough that they had recaptured the ability to do so collegially. The applications would follow.

"We have our own little voyage to complete tomorrow," Marion segued, patting him on the calf. "I hope the weather will be okay."

"It will be fine," Adam predicted, "quite fine. On that score I disagree with Mr. Ramsay."

Still bagged in clear plastic, Adam examined the cut halves of his sandwich—a lowly PB&J today, since they had consumed most of the perishable fodder—inspecting them for damage incurred in transport; he then removed the one that appeared more rumpled and, with a smart wrist-snap, a catcher's toss back to the mound, sailed it far enough out over the bluff to watch a trio of gulls contend over it after it landed. Earlier a handful of cashews had been apportioned to the same fate. Initially indifferent, but now moved to vexation by the perception of waste, Marion rose to the bait. "What are you doing?" she demanded.

He had been anticipating the question. "I suspect I'm saving the life of a minnow or two, upholding the bottom of the food chain. Just think of it: indirectly, my little gift to the birds helps sponsor a tuna steak."

Within his mood she detected a vague unworldliness, an element of detachment. Occasionally he did this: stepped back from himself and analyzed the implications of his actions, their fit within the greater scheme. She could only respect him for it; he did not come by his faults unawares. "You're not hungry?" she pursued.

"Oh, but I am." The paradox, he knew, would nettle her.

On his face she observed what seemed an expression of suppressed excitement, the signature of some withheld news. Pretending not to, she warned, "I'm not sharing any of mine," as, ordinarily, she would have: toward the end of many meals, he became, by proxy, her chick, her nestling; maternally, she could not resist the call of self-sacrifice, the urge to transfer succor, a symbolic morsel, to his plate.

How to explain himself? he wondered. Incredulously, across a pearly inner horizon, he had been witnessing the dawn of a new capability. Heretofore unachievable, willpower, a capacity for abnegation, was arising within him. As certainly as bone or muscle, he could feel its heft, its flex and usability. He took a bite out of the remaining half, then jettisoned this, too. "The body is highly efficient," he advocated. "That should hold me until dinner."

Our human ties are forever subject to rebalancing, a restless algebra of progress and disappointment. Closing her eyes, Marion held them shut long enough to allow for a minor recalibration of assumptions. After years of chiding him to eat less, she had finally come to accept that he would always carry a thumb's breadth of insulation, and treble that over the tenderloins. Yet it is only when we cease investing in a wish that it may be granted, only when we despair of change that it ensues. Her first response to his display of abstemiousness was cautious and skeptical. "You don't want to let yourself get too hungry; you might overindulge tonight."

Guilty images of second and third helpings and clandestine snacks filtered in. "That's been my problem," he acknowledged. "I haven't known how to check myself."

"And now?"

"Now I see that I must counter one appetite with another."

Again the mystical tone.

"Hear me out." Raising his hand, he made the "halt" sign. "Would you agree that one can develop a taste for things, find them more appealing over time?"

"Of course."

"And that we can learn to like what, at first, held little interest?"

"Yes."

"Is there any reason, then, why this should only apply to externals? In our experience of ourselves, can we not acquire a preference for a particular attitude or state of being? Along the way can't we discover the value of solitude or hopefulness or independent thinking?"

The droning surf and importuning wind helped advance his case. Flux, they seemed to remind her, was the only given. She should not discount the possibility, within the character of her spouse, of some limited reform. "I'm sure we can," she admitted.

Adam peered out over the gathering chop, toward the convergence of ocean and sky. "I think something like that is happening to me," he said, speaking in a level, preoccupied tone. "Restraint, that's what it is. I think I'm developing an appetite, a desire, for restraint."

Judiciously, she gave this announcement time to settle, to weigh in the balance. To be sure, there would have been a time when she would have scoffed, diagnosing it as a ploy, or at best, a short-lived flare of good intent, but now the instinctive faculty within her that measured and sifted the quality of things produced a different take: by her intuition, this was real; in the daily labor of self-regulation, Adam had stumbled upon a better grip, an improved handhold. Further, she thought, this is just what happy, well-seasoned couples do: in their maturity they offer small gifts of temperament to each other; they become neater, less judgmental, more earnestly kind; they deliver on a few of the neglected or broken promises. Perhaps he would not succeed with this; perhaps his drive for thinness would flag, or his method would fail. Still, other concessions floated within their reach. He would make some, and she would make others. Ahead, she saw only a smoother path, more harmonious days. "Why, that's wonderful, darling," she praised him. "You'll fit back into your old tuxedo. We'll have to go out dancing!"

The rain, she saw, was almost upon them. In anticipation of it they had repaired to the house, retreated under cover. Looking out from the porch, Marion observed curtains of heavy precipitation, a torrential leading edge, approaching the island; soon, they would be hit with a downpour. As a child, she had been restless and fretful at the advent of storms; behind every lightening bolt and thunderclap that cleaved the Midwestern sky, she had imagined, lurked the wrath of a distempered deity: a jilted Zeus, a vengeful Thor. Neither had it helped that at "Country Day" she had been regularly subject to disaster-drilling—a concession to the occasional, maverick tornado which strayed into the outskirts of Lake Forest from the natal prairies further west—nor that a second cousin had once perished in a hurricane. As a result, in these portentous moments before weather struck, a craven reflex asserted itself, and though she did not literally cower, she did suffer, under the whip strokes of anxiety, a defeat of the spirit. She could feel it coming on now: the dry-throatedness, the hollowed-out sensation in her gut, the fluttering, subsidiary rhythm within her pulse. Presently she would be in the thrall of angst. *If I'm going to do this,* she forced herself to think, *it's time to proceed. What do the shrinks call it— implosion? Better yet, in this case, immersion. So then:* with a fortifying gasp, she lifted off her blouse.

"What are you doing?"

Though Adam was in the living room, lounging on the couch, the question sounded almost instantaneously. Truly, men possess a special sense which, even at a distance, alerts them to impending nudity. "Something I need to do," she confessed. "Something I'll be better for."

From his position, Adam could see only his wife's untanned torso; the rest was blocked by interposed structures: a table, a lamp shade.

After the bra came off she stood stock-still for a second in what could have been a modeling pose. Classically proportioned, her figure, he thought, could have stood in for any of the famous Venuses; she gave nothing up to Botticelli or Milo. Proudly, he hailed, "You grace the scene, darling. You make a delightful apparition."

She was too engaged in the effort of revving her will to offer repartees or explanations. The storm, the urgency of the moment, was beckoning; she was determined to heed its call. In a voice that seemed dislocated from itself, the product of ventriloquy, she asked, "Will you get a towel for me, dear? I'll need one when I get back."

He was still rising from his seat when he heard the screen door fling open, and by the time he arrived at the threshold of the porch, his wife, in the guise of a manic nymph, was scurrying naked over the rocks, rushing to meet the squall. She seemed to reach her destination, a great oblong boulder that resembled the leg of a fallen dolmen, just in time to climb up on it and stretch out her arms in a gesture of supplication before she was inundated. And as the tempest closed over her he could only guess at what antic or deranged purpose had drawn her out into that cold rain, but afterwards, shivering but exultant—and safe again in his arms—she would describe it like this:

"Hello.... Burr.... Oh good, you found a beach towel.... Ah, that's better...wrap me up...mmm, keep rubbing.... That's good. ... Brings the blood back to your skin.... Well, you must think me a s-silly girl, running amok like that...but it was wonderful, really it was.... I'm going to do it every time there's a cloudburst and there's nobody around. It's like being born to a new part of yourself; it's just you and nature and nothing in between. You take the energy in without being afraid of it. You feel cleansed and re-v-vitalized.... Oh, that's it, put your arms all the way around me...tighter...ah.... There, that's good."

The story, she realized, had come too far, too fast. It could not be parceled into dithering, Victorian installments; it should not be rendered piecemeal. For best effect, moreover, it should be told in reverse, leading backwards from the denouement. "I'm in love again!" she foresaw herself confiding in a husky whisper, leaning forward at their regular Thursday lunch.

Dubiously, Judy would ask for clarification: "With?" (Judy was her primary confidante; she had long been aware their marriage had staled.)

"With Adam." She would beam, her visage filling with a confirming flush. Yet the art of that conversation would be to steer her friend away from the whys and wherefores, any detailed explication. For she had lost track of most of it herself. The individual, successive steps in her reconciliation with Adam had become a muddle in her mind, a daisy chain unstrung. And, curiously, she believed that was the very proof: True love is powerless to dissect itself. Just as much, it is private; it must preserve its secrets.

These two letters, then, would not go ashore. They would join a lost body of literature, all those heartfelt missives that are reconsidered, held up, never sent. Crumpling one in each hand, she tossed them into the fire that had been lit to warm her. Happy news, she thought, is its own exegesis. The more scant the commentary, the sweeter the tale.

Louise Falk had never been one to go in for omens. To the extent that she attempted to predict the future, or divine the unseen, it was solely on the basis of reasoned inference: what a formation of clouds tells of the impending weather, what a sequence of bids implies about the location of trump. More particularly, she had always scoffed at the notion of signs in nature, Wordsworthian intimations received along the riverbank; in her book the poetic fallacy was simply that.

Yet if once a skeptic on the subject, Louise, these days, is more open-minded, less doctrinaire. Cautiously, she will admit that it is possible for us to achieve a connectedness, a concordance, with the environment, and that from this link we may receive foreshadowings, a slim prefiguration of things to come.

What is the source of her new perspective? She credits simply what she calls her "experience." One Saturday afternoon in June she was at her usual routine, sipping a shorty on the terrace and waiting for Ed to come home from the club. (Seventy-four and retired, he was still striving for the duffer's last hurrah: shooting his age.) For days it had been hot and muggy, the air thick with grit; aberrant for Connecticut, it was the type of weather that fosters domestic strife, rash acts. Having endured it initially, she was beginning to succumb. That morning she had been curt to the housekeeper, snippy to a deliveryman. Worse, she could feel her peevishness escalating. Soon, she would have to reach for the Valium. Either that or catch a flight to Banff. And that night she was going to *insist* that Ed put in a pool.

In hindsight, Louise thinks of all that horrible heat and humidity as a necessary preface to what followed. For to perceive figure we must have ground. Those suffocating conditions, she believes, were a kind of tabula rasa onto which a sign, an augury, was etched. "Imagine yourself as I was that evening," she would tell you, "then picture this: the first thing I noticed was the noise of the insects—suddenly, there wasn't any. Next, the air grew fresher and lighter; all the grime seemed to drop out of it. Then I felt the nearness of something. Do you know how you can sometimes tell you're not alone? You turn around, and a person who hasn't announced himself is there, and in the moment just before you see him you can feel his presence. That's how it was. I felt an essence, the suchness of something, close by. And it was then that I knew. I realized that they would be all right, that they were working it out. And they have, as you can see. But I knew it back then, months ago, when they were still on that island, before their announcement. Just a mother's intuition, was it? I doubt it. To me it was something more than that. A glimpse through the looking glass."

"I like your outfit."

"Why, thank you, darling."

"What made you choose it?"

It was the cocktail hour. On the porch, seated at right angles around a low, Plexiglass table, they were watching a clearing wind doing its work, dispatching a flank of remnant clouds. At first she took his inquiry casually. "It's one of my standard combinations," she told him. "I'm sure you've seen it before." With a playful, lilting gesture she held her arms out to her side, inviting his inspection. She wore a cerise top over black jeans; above her neckline, strands of Cartier gold, the tithe from their tenth anniversary, shimmered.

"Let me modify the question," he said, setting down his drink. "Red is such a strong color. What would it imply if you were wearing, say, beige instead?"

Where was he going with this? She felt like a passenger in a vehicle that has abruptly turned off the familiar road onto a narrow, rutted, overgrown lane. "Well"—she balked, not immediately retrieving an insight—"I suppose it would mean I was in a more subdued mood."

Nodding, he allowed himself an aliquot of satisfaction. Little used, his intuition had passed the first test. "I would have guessed as much," he said. "And the red? Does it indicate that that you're feeling on your game tonight?"

This probative dialogue was a new mode for them. To prepare for it, Marion reset her haunches, leaned more towards him, and prematurely stubbed out her cigarette. These inaugural questions, she sensed, were akin to the initial moves of a seduction; he now wanted her permission to continue, to press his case. "That's pretty accurate," she admitted, raking her forelocks back. It was a mannerism she tended to employ, as if to clear the incidental clutter from her mind, when a topic of interest had unexpectedly crept up on her. "I do feel rather zesty. Why the quiz?"

Admiringly, Adam studied his wife's high-bred features; throughout their range of expression they remained subtly drawn, artfully configured. "We have more knowledge of each other than we think," he proposed, "but less than we should have. There's the paradox, and there's the challenge."

Around them the sibilance of the wind and the commotion of the trees seemed to subside. "I'm listening," she said.

Adam clasped his hands in his lap, then offered a promise, a penance. "I want to transpose myself into you," he said. "I want to understand how the world looks from your side, how you experience things—every whim and whimsy, every desire, every need. I'll be a better husband for it."

He was right, of course. What was still lacking between them, as it was between most couples, was fully developed empathy, phenomenological permeability between their two beings. There are parts of the self that are more private than the flesh; they are the last things we undrape as we unite. Until then we guard them with silence and dissimulation and humor. To seize the moment she must abandon these defenses; to be completely married she must withdraw all the bolts, open the latches, let him in. Quietly, she told him, "I would like that. And it will be mutual?"

"Entirely."

Diffidently, they paused, awaiting, it seemed, a quickening of their bodies, some permissive shift of biochemistry that would allow them to engage each other fully, put everything forth. They were at the point of broaching a frontier, the existing limit of their ability to trust. To proceed from here, however falteringly, would be a species of valor.

"How do we go about this?" she asked. Askance, she took in his attentive bearing, his earnest mien.

"My idea," he said, "is that we don't stop at the *what;* we should always try to get to the *why*: why we prefer one thing—a style of writing, an arrangement of furniture—over another. To love a person competently is to understand the subjectivity behind all their choices, to try on their philosophy of being."

"You flatter me, darling. I don't think there's any such coherence about me. I'm a smorgasbord."

Tenderly, he persevered. "A collage perhaps—we all are. What I want to know is why every piece sits where it does, how it supports the whole."

She found his metaphor apt. It took in the notion that design can exist beneath superficial disorder. Indeed, that was how she saw herself, her personal story, mostly: as a kind of action painting, a series of bold strokes drawn from the heart. If he could embrace all the errant loops, the seemingly stray marks, it would fortify her soul. Tolerance, she thought, the amused acceptance of another's interior foolishness, is the final stage of commitment. After twenty-odd years, they were close to attaining it. "Very well," she resolved, "I'll go first." Arising in unison from her sides, her hands made a helpless, ironic splaying gesture. "Have I ever told you why I like to leave the windows in our bedroom open?"

It had always been a minor annoyance, her need to draft in the outside air, even in the depths of winter. "Because you sleep better that way, I presume."

"No, that's not the reason." To facilitate her confession, Marion peered into the shadows building in the nearby groves. As the dark looms we speak more easily of the irrational. "It's for the house fairies."

Her tone had become sheepish, beguiling, pre-adolescent—the voice of an eight-year-old confiding an imaginary friend, or the wizardly powers of a favorite toy. Instinctively he felt protective: she was entrusting to him her "inner child," her primitive self. Gently, he urged, "Tell me, please."

As a little girl, she had lived in rooms teeming with puckish spirits, the unlicensed creations of Hedel, a lumbering and emphysematous Austrian widow her parents had retained as a nanny. Unable to physically keep after Marion and her brothers, Hedel had installed a legion of wee deputies throughout the Scott household, invisible sentinels invested with the power to impose eccentric and fanciful punishments—an intractable itch, persistent hiccups—on bad behavior; thus, the house fairies. "It's one of those things you're told when you're young," she explained, "that you never really stop believing. The woman who used to watch us turned Hans Christian Anderson against us. She had us convinced she was being assisted by sprites; they supposedly needed the windows open so they could return to their homes after we were asleep."

"And one doesn't want to spite a sprite."

"Precisely."

"That's a charming little foible, my dearest, now that I know where it comes from. You should have told me sooner."

She scanned his features to see if he meant it: his lips, yes, had turned up at the corners. "As you know," she baited, "I have many more."

Here was the vindication, he mused, in being wedded to a neurotic, a slightly nicked and dented soul. Many years into it, you were still engaged in an intimate form of archeology, uncovering explanatory fragments, missing shards; as the pieces were assembled, you appreciated, more and more, the elegance of the faience, the uniqueness of its design. "We'll get to them all," he promised her, "mine as well as yours."

And as he predicted, they did, over the next few months, unearth everything: all their unspoken fears, suppressed desires, close-held fantasies. In the process they were reminded that there is no such thing as an uncomplicated psychology. Moreover, they succeeded in setting aside certain long-held assumptions, particularly the notion that there is a limit to our human ties, our ability to achieve a sympathetic interconnectedness. For this, at the point where they had imagined it, they had already managed to exceed.

Though entirely pleasant, their dinner that night bore a different subjectivity.

Consider, for example, one's dream of a walk through the woods as it would compare to the actuality. In the dream there is a presumption of light-footedness, of being able to make one's way without effort, free from resistance; in reality there is undergrowth that impedes, roots that confound.

Their previous meals had scarcely seemed to require any input, any earnest labor; this one entailed the usual prefatory steps, the ordinary mundanities.

They heard the clacking and jangling of pans; they felt the slither of raw filets; they saw the soup splatter.

This meal they *made.*

But in making it they had the sense of carrying out some obscure or half-forgotten tutelage, of acting under guidance. For Marion, though she had never attempted lobster bisque before, inexplicably knew the recipe; and Adam, though he had never prepared julienne vegetables before, sliced the carrots and celery to perfection.

It was as if the menu choice and the knowledge of how to proceed had been instilled in them through a lesson which, in itself, they could no longer recall.

More broadly, in the months after that, they would sustain a belief that they had somehow been reschooled while they were on the island, a conviction that a potency unknown to them had ushered them forward towards a kinder, more adaptable, more resilient version of themselves.

To this very moment they see those seven days as an inflection point, a time when an extrinsic force, a guiding hand, lifted them up. Yet whenever they try to look back and probe the mechanism, the provenance, of their recovery, their remembrance clouds at the center. Though they can clearly recall the first few hours and the last, some part of what lies between—and in certain of these pages— remains lost to them. Mostly it seems like a story they tried to overhear but couldn't, loose ends of a conversation divided by a gust of wind across the beach which sweeps the words away.

His fingers upheld a smoky image rendered in aquamarine. "Disco: Quintet *Québécois*," the caption read. Once they had ventured into such a place. Just off the Boulevard St. Germain, a few steps down from street level: *Club Zed.* He recalled a long, cavernous room with simple chairs and a curving banquette at one end, a low band platform at the other; on one side there had been a bar ensconced in an alcove, but the remaining area, the approximate volume of a mobile home, had been open, a space capable of accommodating a dozen-odd pairs, a *douzaine* nimbly pirouetting couples.

At the Swing, alas, no less than any other genus of dance, he had proven maladroit. Inevitably, he fumbled the spins, bollixed the pretzels. His timing was errant; his movements were balky. Yet it was not for a lack of trying. Over the years he had done the duty at all too many soirées, scuffed ankles with a generation of table partners. And the lessons that Marion had inveigled him into—twice—had scarcely had an impact. Constitutionally, he lacked the genes for rhythm, for fluidity and grace of movement. *But for one brief moment,* he resolved, *why not just pretend?* Cannily, he opened the jewel case, slipped the disc onto the tray.

"What are you up to, baby?"

"I though we'd have a little music on our last night, something to get us back into the tempo of civilization." It was the first time either of them had sifted through the owners' CD collection; their states of mind earlier in the week—misery, then anxious uncertainty—had suppressed their interest.

Marion was finishing up at the counter, balancing the last of the dinner pots on the drying rack. Cheerfully, she told him, "I'll go for a little jazz, if they have it."

He pressed the wedge on the console marked "play;" obediently, the machine swallowed his selection, then groaned as if suffering the digital equivalent of indigestion. At the end of a pause he heard the click of drumsticks signaling the beat, followed by a salvo of guitar notes. "Simone" was a springy, self-assured tune, rippling with energy. He felt the first clarinet riff pass sensuously through him, tickling his cells. He had always savored music, always been viscerally affected by it. That he was so inept at it, neither able to carry a note nor play an instrument, had always struck him as unjust, a misallocation of talent by the Fates. "How will this do?" he asked.

The sway in her torso, the incipient sluing in her hips gave approval. She seized the two ends of her dish towel and held them stiff-armed in front of her, stand-ins for a partner's hands. Her eyes closed, retaining behind them the image of some perfect, glittery moment, some synchronous bliss. It was his cue: as much as any woman ever is, she was ready to be whisked away, mastered, owned. He approached her from behind and preemptively grabbed the cloth. "May I cut in?"

She looked back at him with the type of expression which, for a man, is nearly as gratifying as the opportunity to which it subsequently leads. "I'd be entirely charmed," she averred. There was no reserve in her tone, no overlay of skepticism; her cognizance of his awkwardness seemed to have been beneficently suspended. Confidingly, she added, "For you, I'm always available."

As he remembers it now, it was just at that point that he caught hold of something outside of himself, a thread of spontaneity. He let it pull his body and hers through a series of smoothly linked turns, into a new range of aptitude. And for a moment, at the apogee, he sensed it: what it is to be unselfconsciously on the beat—a dancer. It did not last, of course; it was merely a brief glimpse into what he might have been in a different incarnation. But for him—for them—it was sufficient. For at last they had held the touchstone; for an instant they were weightless, exultant, free.

The sea that night, freshly rinsed by the afternoon's deluge, presented a relaxed countenance, low swells easing by beneath a platinum sheen. Seen from a slight elevation, its surface resembled the moonstruck expanse of adjacent bedspread he would habitually monitor during boyhood, awaiting sleep. Then and now, he had always found these luminous nocturnal vistas provocative; they constituted an interface between this world and some other; they were glazed by myth. Yet if across the tableau of his repose he had hypothesized a migration of elves or the gambolings of Lilliputians, he could not concoct such pleasant company from this vantage. Rather, lying in wait for him beneath the slumbering ocean, it was the leviathan that he envisioned, that fell creature we encounter far from daylight, the nub of dread, the distillation of all our fears. *All your life,* he thought, studying the chosen point of entry, *you've needed to do this.*

Standing beside him, Marion spoke matter of factly of the logistics. "We can get out over here," she proposed, aiming the beam of her flashlight towards a small shelf at the waterline.

He had to marvel at her gameness, her pluck. She no longer seemed daunted by the dark and the deep; now the ambiguities of nature called up something in her that was beautifully untamed. "I have to thank you for agreeing to this little excursion," he said. "I thought you might nix the idea."

She looked at him sidewise through the brackish air and demurred. "Of course not, sweetheart. This is just the sort of crazy little outing that I adore."

To join in someone else's risk, to take up their folly, is comradeship, is love. A week ago, he knew, she would have balked. Setting their adventure in motion, he dropped his towel onto the rocks and shouted a boisterous invocation to the stars: "On with it, then!" Nimbly, he made his way down a short declivity to the proposed point of exit and inspected it. "It's not too slippery," he declared; "we should have no trouble coming out. We're lucky it's nearly high tide. I'll leave my light here as a mark. Spot me on the way up, will you?"

Watching the deliberate, spidery motions of his ascent, Marion glossed to *The Metamorphosis* and conceived a sequel: "Mr. and Mrs. Adam Falk awoke one morning from uneasy dreams to find themselves transformed in their bed into giant insects." In her version, there would be no guilt, no shame, no hiding away. Though changed into arachnids, she and Adam would live out their lives unshrinkingly; their affection, their ardor, for each other would not falter. Metaphorically, the work would uphold the dignity of aging lovers; it would rebuff the vanity of youth.

Back beside her, Adam took the flashlight and reexamined the landing zone: the drop-off, he confirmed, was steep; perched nine or ten feet above the surface, they should easily be able to clear the bluff. "I'll go first," he told her. "Don't forget to jump as far out as you can."

She pressed an index finger reprovingly to his ribs. "Dearest, I'm the one who's had the diving instruction, remember?"

He smiled distractedly. Distractedly because his consciousness had now gone ahead of itself; already it had endured the wanton rasp of sharkskin, the merciless first bite. As they disrobed, he did so with a sense of solemnity, of participation in the sacrificial. His incongruous nakedness afoot this stony precipice felt atavistic. He was prepared to be anointed and saved; just as well, he was prepared to meet a thankless oblivion. Either way, he would accept the outcome as definitive, a proper verdict on the question of his adequacy, his manhood. "Make sure that I'm out of the way before you come in," he reminded her, approaching the edge. Then, with a final fortifying gasp, he was off, hurtling through the obsidian night. The interval to impact persisted longer than he expected, allowing him to preview a more concussive, perhaps tidier fate—his skull dashed, his neck unhinged—before his body sliced, unharmed, into the Bay.

That we fear more, or credit less, what we cannot see is a mandate of the instincts. And if our proclivity to doubt, to cringe before the negative assumption, is to be overruled, this can only be through an initiative of the spirit, the will channeled by reason. Why he should be so petrified to reenter the same body of water that he had sported in by daylight was a conundrum, a contradiction. The Jungians, he knew, would profess that it was not *his* anxiety alone: from Grendel to Nessie, the collective unconscious abounds with sea monsters. Yet even if some component of his fright was genetic, a borrowing from the ancestors, the rest, indisputably, was cowardice, a cancer upon his soul. His objective tonight, it had appeared to him, though modest, was straightforward. Though a man cannot quantify terror, or the degree of its subsidence, he can mark time. Ten minutes, he had decided, would be a fitting achievement. If he could remain in the unlit ocean during that span and effect a show of insouciance....that would be enough.

The volumes around him, when he opened his eyes, were not absolutely blank. To his surprise they were strewn with blue-green particles. *Phytoplankton. Photoluminescence.* From introductory biology, out of extended dormancy, the terms bobbed back into view. Then others: *diatom; echinoderm; zoospore.* Ah, the utility of the inner monologue! Could he employ it to defer panic just as he— sometimes—delayed climax? A moot point it became, for his arm, in reaching to carve out a stroke, contacted something elongated and slick, serrated, rubbery. Though he knew it to be seaweed he recoiled, thrashing about as if combating an eel, a tentacle. Once free, he jetted desperately to the surface.

Above, the world seemed to have reverted to prehistory. Uncounted but surely more numerous, as yet unclaimed by astronomy, the stars overarched what appeared to be a more vast sky. Behind him the island loomed barbaric, a jagged monolith dividing the primal soup. It was a scene from the inchoate planet, the time before Time. Never before had he felt so cut off from human notice, the prospect of clemency. Acutely he perceived himself to be mortal, earth-bound, infinitesimally small. What we all are: mere jots of protoplasm. Oh, we scurry and squirm and cavil and fornicate—but to what end? Does any of it make us worthier than the paramecium? And by what logic do we alone claim hope of resurrection, of a continuance? No, he resolved, if he was to remain in this life, it would be by virtue of relinquishing such hubris. He and the petrels and the bluefish: henceforth they would all be on equal footing, each mere wisps in the deity's dream. Perhaps the Hindus, the Buddhists had it right: it is through at-oneness that we conquer fear. And so, tentatively, he tried it. Head back, spread-eagling, he took a breath and held it, putting himself into a drift. Belly-up, he lay inert in the water. Flotsam. Sargasso. Of a kind with all insensate things. But still a part of it: yes. Still a datum, a fact, of this precious world. Regardless of the incarnation, it was splendid just to *be*. For somehow, it had to have been sponsored. These lulling tides, these stolid shores, this air, this night, this firmament: it was entirely a craftwork, he saw. Not happenstance, not randomness. And then he actually relaxed. Exhaled, inhaled. Laughed. Raucous and unrestrained, his voice lifted over the hiss of the surf, reverberated off the headland. Soon, it found accompaniment. Giggling, Marion pulled up to him through the water, tugged at his arm, and asked, "What have you found that's so amusing out here, you silly man?"

He continued to float, to meditate. His mind held to an Eastern tranquility. "Everything, darling," he said at last. "The wonder and the absurdity. The spectacle of the cosmos. All creation."

SUNDAY

Barely astir, there seemed something confectionary about this early morning air. A whiff of peppermint? A hint of peach? A pleasing scent regardless, perhaps given off by shy corollas that would soon close, immuring themselves against the returning sun. With a prolix inspiration Marion drew it in, arching her shoulders back to increase her take. "Everything's so fresh at this hour," she said, speaking softly, reverently. "I'm glad we got up when we did."

Adam's eyes remained trained on the horizon, the roseate onset of day. For several minutes he had been watching the continuous flux among the bands of colors there; he was new to the realization that time is liquid, that at its edges you can watch it flow. "It's something to relish," he agreed. "The atmosphere is so clear; every detail is available."

They were seated on a commodious rock halfway down the lee slope of the island. A desultory stroll had brought them only a short distance from the house, to this representative vista. Across the Bay the impassive silhouettes of the nearby islands languished mutely on a lavender bed. It was their final opportunity to register the beauty of the place without distraction; in three hours the launch would be arriving to transport them back to the mainland and, in the interim, they had to have breakfast, clean up, and finish packing.

Marion pointed towards a lone cormorant skimming the water beneath them. "Listen. You can even hear its pinions touching."

It was true: though the bird was at least fifty yards away, he was able to make out a short, percussive sound at the end of each wing beat. "It opens up your senses to be out in nature," he said.

Marion peered up into the deep blue sky and the realm beyond. "I don't think it's just that."

"Oh?"

"To see the world in all its glory: it's what our being in love—again—allows."

"Ah. Yes. Certainly. I agree."

There is a solemn, consecratory quality to the last meal we take before leaving a special place. While we gather our concluding impressions, a respectful reflex bids us to remain hushed and meditative. Already the nostalgia builds.

For the Falks, the occasion carried a double valence. Not only were they about to leave the island; also it was time to clinch their understanding of what had happened there. Intuitively, they both felt a need to sum up, attest, conclude. The recrudescence of their romance, that is, was still on the order of a lottery win, an extraterrestrial visit. It wafted through their awareness as something breathtaking and miraculous, yet unconfirmed. To authenticate it they had to hold it up to the light, turn it round and round, swear by what they saw.

Marion initiated, "Would you have ever believed this was possible?" Possessively, she placed her palm on his forearm and slid it down over his hand; briefly their wedding rings clacked.

As he considered his response he studied her facial tone, the presumptions set into her features. Her lips, he noted, were full and slack; gone was the slight pucker that formed with any ambivalence or discontent. Her cheeks, too, looked pink and succulent. This was the same ripeness, he perceived, the same luscious complexion that had held him in its thrall on a humid spring day half a lifetime ago, when they had exchanged vows before a packed house in a vermillion-carpeted, excessively gilt Presbyterian church in east Lake Forest. Ethan Cowes, a reedy, narrow-eyed actuary-turned-minister had presided. Outside, a threatened thunderstorm had auspiciously dissipated. The reception had been held at Gatsby's other home, a stucco mansion surmounting a vast, close-cut lawn overlooking Lake Michigan. For their wedding pictures they had chosen, as backdrop, its steady cobalt hue. "I felt pretty beaten down when we arrived here," he admitted. "What's taken place between us has to be quite rare."

She turned his hand over and, with her forefinger, slowly traced out his lifeline. It was a novel intimacy for her, an addition to a repertoire which, in the coming months, would be extensively refurbished. "The stars were aligned for us, weren't they?"

"Yes."

At a minimum they would continue to believe at least this much. Whatever interpretations they might later attempt, whatever speculations they might put forth, this appraisal, this conviction, would persist. And though the text of the just-passed week had already been emended, necessarily leaving them with imperfect recollections of what transpired between the opening and the denouement, they would take it as given that the action in the middle was special: providential. Henceforth they would hold to the notion that we do not inhabit an indifferent world, an aimless scheme; that to the presiding influences we are somehow of consequence.

"I hope that we get it right this time." Yet even in voicing doubt she knew that they would. We are never so appreciative as when we are given a second lease. Nothing is presumed; all is savored. Our gratitude revises us.

"I don't know what we've done to particularly deserve this," he reflected, "but perhaps that's the point: we're all potentially redeemable."

He paused, letting the thought settle. Their eyes roamed—met. And then, gratuitously, it resumed. The static. The flow. The last thing that had been missing. So long absent, their entire troth, their venture into matrimony had rested on this. From the beginning it had been a question of biophysics. The process was palpable, liquid, osmotic. To each it provided what they themselves lacked. They remembered the sensation now: what it was like when all the orbitals were filled in, all the electrons spun.

"What were you saying?"

"It's not important."

And truly it wasn't, for alongside their conversation they were holding a parallel exchange, a wordless dialogue. The contents of that communication are privy, the property of the heart, yet suffice it to say that it involved an agreement that the design that had brought them to the island had succeeded at its work, that a bright and unsuspected kismet had been fulfilled.

"Adam, feel this."

Their bags were packed; the bed had been stripped. Now they were sorting the leftovers into two garbage bags: one for trash, one to be brought home. Marion was holding one of the plain loaves they had brought along as fodder.

He touched, squeezed. His fingers met a soft, springy texture. Curious, he took it from her and held it; it seemed almost weightless.

"It's still fresh."

"How can that be?"

It was a question neither one of them could manage to answer.

The launch was regrettably punctual in coming for them. They would not have minded, to be sure, had it been delayed by some glitch in the mechanics or tardiness by the operator, for they were at the point where it was just hitting them: the finality of departure, the nearness of ordinary life. Such is the backlash of all the best getaways: the greater the remove, the more jarring the return.

"I'm afraid this is our ride," said Adam.

Steady on its course, entraining a passel of opportunistic gulls above its wake, the same blue-hulled bass boat that had brought them out was closing on the breakwaters.

"It should be a smooth trip in," Marion consoled, latching her hand to his shoulder. They were standing at the end of the floating dock; for the past few minutes they had been engaged in a mesmeric vigil, earnestly trying to take it all in—the crystal-pure air, the tranquil seascape. No breeze had yet developed; no commotion presented itself. They were free to peruse the world in a state of placidity, to find it good.

"When we get back into the range of reception," Adam said, "we should call the kids. We've been out of touch all week."

A Cheshire cat smile formed on Marion's lips. "Sometimes parents need to do that."

"*We* certainly did."

"What shall we tell them?"

He fitted his arm around her waist, then nuzzled along her forehead, imparting the slightest kiss. Freshly rinsed, her hair held a fine, complicated fragrance, the scent of lemon bedded in mink. "Oh," he considered, "not very much. They're pretty perceptive; they'll pick up on the change of tone."

She turned and raised her gaze to look upon him, discerning once more, in the distance between the high forehead and the prominent jaw, in the Anglo-Saxon visage perhaps slightly coarsened by some unacknowledged Celtic or Teutonic strain, an authentic American construction, her bonny original man. Within the range of his vision, she trusted, within the reach of those army-green eyes, there lay a future to be believed in, promises that would be kept. "Do you suppose our friends will also?"

It struck him that there would be gospel to disseminate when they returned, the word about themselves. This much they owed to their circle, to any couple within it that might be flagging. "We'll have to make sure they do," he said, cinching her in.

Love is exultant; love is proud. Yet just as much, love is generous. Its seeks to pay dividends; it aims for distribution. Endorsing the sentiment, she told him, "Yes, we must."

The boat was upon them now, breaching the jetties, throttling down. It looped through the moorings and coasted towards them in a perfect curve, measuring the dock as a tangent. In the cockpit they recognized Mrs. Judkins and—Chris, was it?—the laconic skipper.

"Don't you real-estate types ever get a day off?" Adam quipped as the fenders were about to touch.

"Not very often, during the season!" Floating above her plumpish physique, the woman's features—pudgy cheeks, rouged lips, dark, ringleted hair—seemed cartoonish and oversimplified. Her squeaky voice and hot-pink sweater magnified the effect. She was Betty Boop in Topsiders, comedic-persona-meets-Sotheby's-Realty. "But I don't mind coming to the office," she appended, turning and holding her arms up to the view.

It had been a week since they had conversed with anyone except each other. The process felt clumsy and effortful, particularly with this gabby saleswoman. Away from civilization, how quickly we lose our social edge, our facility for being glib. Taking her turn at the pleasantries, Marion put in, "Well, you're looking at two satisfied customers! We've had a *glorious* time here! Do you *have* to bring us back?"

Mrs. Judkins shifted her feet and stood with arms akimbo, as if this were her stock position for accepting praise. "I'm so glad you like it. Some people find it a little too remote; for others, it's the perfect escape."

"Count us as 'others,'" Adam grunted, as he stooped to cleat a line. Rising, he added, with more breath, "It was just what we needed." Realtors, he assumed, routinely encountered people involved in happy transitions: marriage, parenthood, new employment. But did they see much of this? He wondered: couples mending, attachments reinstated, futures restored. Certainly more so here than on the typical suburban beat, selling fixer-uppers in Newton, walk-ups in Brookline. Properties here had the potential to prove alembics; they should be touted as such.

Numbly, they handed off their duffels, cast off, and stepped aboard. It all transpired abruptly, anticlimactically. After such a transforming interlude they might have expected an antiphonal chorus, or a whispered benediction, to issue from those accommodating shores, that propitious isle. But the turnarounds we achieve in our lives are scarcely announced by the devices of theater, and it was only the engine's initial, sputtering cough and subsequent, chuffing idle they heard, then the soft slapping of bow waves as the craft eased away, gathering speed.

A departure refines our sense of what it is that we are leaving. As it ensues we struggle to set images and fix conclusions. Seated now and gazing intently sternward, the Falks applied themselves to this effort far out into the bay, throughout a diminuendo of perspectives, until the island was just a verdant splotch, a fuzzy hyphen, poised on the horizon. Without difficulty they would remember its topography: its scraggly granite base, its evergreen mantle, its rough-carved cols and obscure little glens. Just as surely they would remember the morning dew upon the juniper and the goldenrod bending before the sea-breeze and the companionship of ospreys and all the other unscripted beauties of that place. Yet what was already slipping further out of their awareness was a portion of story that had unfolded there: what must remain a sealed text, the narrative to an epiphany. For we are not privileged to range beyond a certain orbit, to exceed ourselves, to see the face of Him. But still we press on, sojourners into the mist, receding from what is known.

ANON

The Falks, by one, are a larger family now. Eleven months ago they had Michael, a fine-looking baby boy. Already he is standing up, melodically babbling, casting food from the feeding tray, distinguishing himself through his repertoire of behaviors, from the spawn of most lost lower species. Adam and Marion dote on him like first-time parents; they are engrossed in watching his development; it is as though they have not experienced it before, not raised other children. Among their more peripheral friends, the speculation persists that the new arrival was "an accident," or even a ploy, for as rumor had it, they were a pair on the brink. Under this theory the child was adduced as a poultice, a snare, a despairing maneuver to hold their union together. Alas, people will always talk, and the truth is not everywhere taken in.

There has been twaddle, too, among those closer to them, but entirely of the approving kind. Variously, they have been amazed, relieved—inspired—to see the Falks carrying on, behaving like newlyweds. All the more so because there appears to be no end to it. Fully two years into their redux, or second wind, or whatever you may call it, the two continue to be observed entwining hands in the grocery aisle, slow-dancing in the pantry, lounging on a single beach towel.

They comport themselves like people who have not been schooled in what is proper conduct for older, settled citizens. And, if anything, the indications are that their love is not merely resurgent, but increasing. Between them there is heat, around them a dense hormonal nimbus. One wants to get caught up in it, to become definitively infected. What they have, of course, is exclusive; it cannot

179

be shared, only imitated. Yet, sweetly, a few of the couples they know are beginning to try: they are tuning their physiques and polishing their words; they are spending more mornings abed and more evenings alfresco. By a degree or two, Quidnunquit itself seems a more enchanted place. There is almost lyricism in the air, the faint arpeggios of harp music. And at twilight, as patches of fog scud across its brackish lawns, it is tempting to surmise the provenance of it all, to infer a congress of sprites, the capering of fairies: what would suffice for the pagan version of this account.

Every couple spins a story, every wedlock presents a tale to tell. The principals of this one would remind you that, apart from certain inherited advantages, they are unexceptional people. They own their share of flaws; they claim no special talents; they remain captive to their idiosyncrasies. Commensurately, throughout much of its course, their marriage was quite ordinary: it was launched in a rush of fervor; over the years it gradually lost its momentum; by its middle phase it had stalled. Yet at this point, they insist, the action finds a novel line. They do not opt out; they do not permit each other compensatory affairs; they do not settle for hollow convenience. Something happens to deflect the inevitable. The text is retouched; the folios are rearranged. To this day they cannot explain it. The mechanism of their revival is opaque to them. They assert only that it was not internal, that it did not derive from their own initiative. A gift, they will have you call it. What it is that may be bestowed upon us by agencies that are redemptive but unknowable. Adam and Marion have concluded that they are out there. And as they look back on that brief vacation, those seven days away when the change in them was wrought, they can almost glimpse an image. Intercalated between the frames of memory they see a glint, a shining but indeterminate form. It is like a meteor tail noticed only at the end of its subsidence, or the sun's brief reflection off a distant, moving surface. They cannot be granted a fuller view, they understand. For our dreams must dim as we awaken, and the powers preserve their mysteries, and angels work subliminally: thence we retain Free Will. Thus no less so than selected members of their family who concurrently, if more ephemerally, were touched by the same visitant, they remain unaware of the robustness of the traffic which descends Jacob's Ladder; that the Heavenly Host may appear to us in whatever guise they deem suitable, however humble, capricious, or droll; and that many among their ranks have been drawn from our own—including a diminutive, quick-witted schoolteacher from Detroit named Clarence Ross, who departed the flesh several decades before the present one.

The atheists, they accept, will scoff at their account; the critics, if it ever published, will shout *deus ex machina*; and the Holy See, if they dare to speak of those simple loaves which seemed to undergo a reversal of spoilage, whose final count seemed to belie how many had been consumed, will decry it as playing loose with sacramentalism. Yet, truly, none of that concerns them. They were never in it for the debate. No narrative can play to every audience. But as yarns go, theirs, at least, offers hope: that our loves may be restored, that our sins may be assuaged. The Falks—now newfound members of a local parish—know this for a fact. They are certain, indeed, that God is immanent. And in such certainty they have discovered their greatest boon. For blessed are they who have not seen, yet believe.

Amen.